Tails of Flame

GERALD HOLT

A JUNIOR GEMINI BOOK

Published in 1995 by
Stoddart Publishing Co. Limited
34 Lesmill Road
Toronto, Canada
M3B 2T6
(416) 445-3333

Canadian Cataloguing in Publication Data

Holt, Gerald
Tails of flame

ISBN: 0-7736-7431-4

I. Title.

PS8565.058T3 1995 jC813'.54 C95-930277-8
PZ7.H65Ta 1995

Cover Design: Brant Cowie/ArtPlus Ltd.
Cover Illustration: Stephen Quick
Computer Graphics: Tannice Goddard/S.O. Networking
Printed and Bound in Canada

Stoddart Publishing gratefully acknowledges the support of the Canada Council, the Ontario Ministry of Culture, Tourism, and Recreation, Ontario Arts Council, and Ontario Publishing Centre in the development of writing and publishing in Canada.

Contents

PART 1

BOMBER PILOT

Chapter 1

The Gas Mask

Tim Athelstan couldn't breathe. He tried to scream, but no sound came. His throat was dry, tight, aching. He was going to die this time, he knew it. He was going to die — like Bits.

He struggled with the thick, black bands that held the mask tautly against his skin — bands as strong as evil witches' fingers.

He pulled, heart racing, a ringing sensation in his ears. Then, with a rush of air, the clammy rubber, wet with sweat, started to come away. He gulped in a lungful of oxygen as he ripped off the mask.

It was always the same — the smelly black rubber clung so tightly that it was like tearing off his own face.

Tim breathed in shuddering gasps as he lay against the pillow. There was no gas mask, really, he knew that, even though he could see nothing in his new bedroom, totally darkened by the blackout curtains drawn across the window. The terrible nightmare that had haunted him when he was younger had returned.

But that awful night in 1940 hadn't been a dream — it had been a living nightmare.

The eerie, moaning wail of the air-raid siren had wakened him. Grabbing his clothes and gas mask, he'd helped Mum as she'd bundled baby Sarah in a blanket. Then, with Bits leading the way, they'd raced down the garden to the Anderson shelter. The night sky was lit by bursting shells, as anti-aircraft guns sought out the Nazi planes bombing London once again.

Dad had urged Mum to move away from the old house in Hampstead, but she didn't want to go. Captain Athelstan was heading a bomb disposal unit in the area, and she wanted to stay near him. Tim didn't want to leave either. They lived close to the Heath, and he loved it when he and Dad went tobogganing on the snowy slopes. There was Whitestone Pond, too, where he sailed his model boat when they took Bits for a walk. Bits was Dad's dog, an old mongrel. Dad said he must have little bits of all the dog breeds in him.

They'd just reached the shelter when Mum thought she heard the air raid warden's rattle, signalling a gas attack. Tim had barely enough time to pull on his mask before the bombs started to fall. Crump! The ground shook, and the dim bulb hanging in the centre of the corrugated metal roof went out. It came on again, flickering, and to Tim it seemed much dimmer than before. He hoped Mum had matches for the candles. Crump! Tim's bunk bed shook. A trickle of earth fell by the door. Bits whined. Tim looked anxiously at his mother.

"That was close, Mum." Tim's voice was muffled and hollow behind the mask.

Mrs. Athelstan nodded but said nothing. She was looking toward the door. The trickle of earth was becoming a steady stream. Bits barked. Then the ground shook and heaved and all was black as Tim was flung through the air, then pressed into the damp, cold earth that formed the floor of the shelter.

He struggled to get up, but something was pressing down on his back. He couldn't breathe. He had to get the mask off! But his arms were pinned underneath him ...

Then strong hands were lifting him, pulling him out of the cold earth and the tangled mess of twisted metal.

"Poor young fella."

Tim tore at the clinging black rubber, and a helping hand ripped the mask from his face. He gulped in the warm September night air.

"You all right, lad?" The air raid warden was shaking the mask. "Lucky we got to you straight away. You could've suffocated in this."

Tim nodded, gulping another lungful of the sweet night air. The garden was bright as day. Someone was crying. It was Mum. Where was she? Then he felt her strong, gentle hand stroke the fair hair away from his forehead as he gazed in horror up the garden.

Their house was sliced in half. Curtains and blackout drapes waved in the glassless, gaping windows, illuminated by flames. His bed hung in the air, swinging dangerously above the hallway. The mattress and bedclothes were gone. There was no sign of the chest of drawers, or the sailboat that had stood upon it. Then, as he watched, the bed fell, sending up a shower of red and orange sparks, like fireworks on Guy Fawkes Night.

"I thought we'd lost you, Tim."

Tim looked away from the burning house. He was desperately trying not to cry. He shuddered. "I couldn't breathe, Mum. I couldn't breathe."

Mrs. Athelstan stroked his forehead soothingly.

"The filter's clogged with earth, missus." The warden shook the mask by its thick rubber straps, then poked at the round metal cover of the filter. "Not completely clogged. But no wonder he felt he couldn't breathe, poor little lad." He shook his head. "Why was he wearing it?"

"I thought I heard the rattle," said Mum.

The warden shook his head. "This was no gas attack, luv, no need for the mask. They dropped land mines and incendiary bombs, like that one."

He pointed to the house. As he did so, the wall of the kitchen collapsed, pots and crockery cascading down in an ear-splitting crescendo, and the bathroom floor above caved in, sending the bath crashing to the ground in a further shower of sparks.

Baby Sarah, her hair matted with mud, clung to Mum, staring wide-eyed at the house and then at the warden holding Tim's mask.

Tim shuddered again and looked at the hole where the shelter had collapsed. He could have been buried in there, like that girl up the road had been buried a month ago. He closed his eyes. Something was wrong. Something was missing. What was it? "Mum! Where's Bits?"

"Oh, no!" Mum took a half-step toward the shelter.

"What's the matter, missus?" The warden looked puzzled. "You said there was just the boy."

"It's my husband's dog. He's had Bits for years."

The warden shook his head. "You mean there's a dog in there?" He shook his head again. "I'll try, but ..."

Fifteen long minutes later, Tim craned his neck to see as the warden re-emerged from the wreckage, holding something close to his chest.

Bits was dead. Tim knew it the moment he recognized the black and white bundle in the warden's arms. Bits's coat was matted and filthy, his tail limp. Tim hugged the old dog and cried, his tears muddying the dirty fur. He wondered if Bits had struggled, trying to breathe. He screwed up his face and screamed through clenched teeth, "I hate you! I hate you, Hitler!"

Now, Tim lay awake and trembling in his darkened room, remembering how, three weeks ago, the horror had repeated itself. A stray bomb, dropped by a Nazi fighter plane heading for home across the English Channel, had hit their second home, a cottage in Chiddingstone.

"It's all right, Tim." His mother's cool fingers gently stroking his forehead calmed his racing heartbeat. "It's all right. We're safe here."

And Tim returned to the present — it was February, 1944. They were in a new home, Bramley Cottage, a house in the heart of Kent, in the village of Medbury, not in Hampstead, and not in the old cottage at Chiddingstone that Dad had found for them.

Tim sighed. Tears welled up, stinging his eyes. Before Dad left, he'd said, "Look after Mum and Sarah for me, Tim." And all Tim could feel right now was fear and anger. Dad was somewhere in Italy. He wouldn't know where they were anymore, wouldn't know that they'd been bombed out again.

Chapter 2

Widdecombe Fair

"Tim! Tim! Where are you?"

Tim was in the back field with his new Medbury friend, Binky, running along the top of a long, high grass-covered mound beneath which potatoes were stored. He jumped, rolling over in the grass as he landed, a parachute billowing out behind him.

"Tim!"

"Coming, Mum."

Binky grinned down at him. "Good landing, Tim. That's how the Spitfire pilots land when they bail out."

Tim grinned back, pushing his straight fair hair out of his eyes. "Can I have another go, Binky?"

"Not now. Your mum's calling you."

Tim nodded, and gazed enviously at the parachute. Binky said it was an enemy flare parachute, dropped from a Nazi plane to light up the ground and show the pilot where he was. Tim had seen them drifting in the night sky during air raids, but he'd never touched one. Mum had told him never to pick up anything, not even the silver strips the enemy planes dropped to confuse the radar. She said some children had had their hands blown off picking up things like that, and others had been blinded.

But Binky said parachutes were all right. He also said he and his sister had collected window, the narrow strips of paper, silver on one side and black on the other, to make Christmas decorations. Lots of people in Medbury had. The decorations looked good mixed in with the coloured paper chains. Sometimes Mum was strange, Tim thought. And she'd been acting really strangely the last two days. Her eyes were often red and her face had a pinched look, her mouth drawn and thin. What was the matter?

Tim shrugged. "'Bye, Binky." He turned and headed across the field to the top of the road. He could see his mother now, at the garden gate. He broke into run.

"Oh, there you are," said Mrs. Athelstan as Tim charged down the pathway. She looked really tired. "Please hurry, Tim. Grandma and Grandpa will be here any minute now, and I want you clean and tidy. Just look at you — your hair's full of grass!" She ran her fingers through the unruly mop. "And look at this pullover!"

Spiky blades of old, dry grass clung to the woollen fibres. "Oh, dear! Your boots! You'll have to clean them immediately. Wait here while I fetch the shoe-box."

Tim waited at the back door. The sturdy black leather boots with their thick toe-caps were muddy. One of the laces was undone.

Mrs. Athelstan came to the kitchen door, a dark brown box with rope handles in her hands. She and Tim had found it under the stairs when they'd moved into the old farm cottage two weeks before. "Now, please hurry, Tim! I did ask you to keep clean."

"Sorry, Mum." Tim opened the box and surveyed the assortment of brushes and polish. "I tried."

Mrs. Athelstan snorted and went inside.

Tim took out the tin of black Nugget polish, and placed his right foot on the grey stone step. He was proud of his boots. Dad had given them to him for his ninth birthday the year before. They were big then and needed cardboard liners to make them fit. Now they fitted perfectly.

There was the shrill toot of a car horn. A black, square-looking car drew up to the gate — Grandpa's Morris Eight.

"Mum! It's Grandma and Grandpa. They're here!" Tim dropped the brush he'd been using and raced down the path.

Grandpa George was climbing out of the car.

"Steady there, lad!" he called.

But it was too late. Tim stepped on the long black bootlace and, with a lurch, sprawled headlong on the gravel path.

A few minutes later, Grandma was swabbing Tim's left knee. It hurt, but in a funny sort of way. It was a nice kind of hurt, as warm water dribbled down his shin.

"There. That looks clean. Dab some iodine on, Enid," Grandma said to Mrs. Athelstan. "I'll do the other knee." She patted the deep, raw graze with a clean piece of cloth.

Tim turned his head. He didn't want to watch as the iodine was applied. He heard the cork pop out of the medicine bottle and smelled the pungent odour of the dark brown liquid. He clenched his teeth but couldn't prevent a gasp as the iodine seemed to burn its way deep into the wounded flesh.

"Brave young soldier you have there, Enid. Hrmph! Reminds me of Will when he was a boy." Grandpa George cleared his throat loudly. "Do you think he might manage a treacle sandwich?"

Tim couldn't believe his ears. He hardly noticed Mum putting iodine on the other knee. All he could think of was treacle. He hadn't had any for ages, with all the food rationing. He grinned over at Grandpa George.

"Aha! I do believe you're going to pull through," Grandpa said, smiling. "But, for a while, you'll look as if you've been in the wars."

Tim smiled. He wouldn't mind looking like he'd "been in the wars." Better still would be really helping fight the war in some way. He'd planted a Victory Garden behind the cottage at Chiddingstone. He'd collected aluminium milk-bottle caps to help make fighter planes. But he didn't think of that as helping, not really — and the bottle caps were cardboard now.

"Close your eyes a minute, Tim." He winced as Mum dabbed more iodine on his forehead. "Good. Now for a cup of tea. I know I can do with one. If you put the kettle on, Mum, I'll tidy up here."

Grandma Rose nodded.

Two cups of tea and three sandwiches later, Tim had almost forgotten his fall. He gazed at the large, shiny tin of Tate and Lyle's Golden Syrup. "Where did you get the treacle, Grandpa?"

"My secret supplier." Grandpa chuckled. "Now, can you eat another?" He stroked his bushy, grey moustache. Tim had often wondered how Grandpa could eat treacle sandwiches without getting it sticky.

"Now, now, George, the boy will be sick," said Grandma. "And what about his dinner?"

Tim looked enviously at his five-year-old sister, still munching happily. He turned to Grandpa, who had one eyebrow raised questioningly. That was another thing Tim wondered about — how did Grandpa raise one eyebrow without raising the other? Tim had tried, standing in front of the mirror. He couldn't do it.

He shrugged. "I think we should leave it for another time, Grandpa."

Grandpa George nodded approvingly. "Good lad." He turned to Mum. "By the way, Enid, did Will ever talk to you about that cousin of his from Canada, my sister Ruby's boy?"

Mum looked down. Tim saw her twisting her napkin, her knuckles white. When she looked up, her face was drawn, and there was a strained look in her eyes. Now Grandma was frowning across the table at Grandpa. What was wrong?

"You mean Bill, Dad?" Mum's voice had a tight edge to it.

Grandpa nodded. "That's him. He always reminds me of that song, 'Widdecombe Fair.'"

"Why, Grandpa?" said Tim.

"Simple, lad. You know the song — *Tom Pearce, Tom Pearce, lend me your grey mare. All along, down along, out along lea.*" Grandpa's voice was rich and mellow. "*For I want to go to Widdecombe Fair — Wi' Bill Brewer, Jan Strewer —*"

"Please, George," Grandma Rose interrupted. "We all know what a marvellous voice you have. Get to the point."

Grandpa cleared his throat noisily. "Thought I was." He turned to Tim. "You see, my sister Ruby married a man called Reg Brewer. He was here, from Canada, during the Great War, the last war, that is. They have just the one boy, Bill Brewer — like the name in the song."

"Oh, I see."

"Anyway," said Grandpa, "I heard from him a couple of days ago. Three days ago, I think. He's here in England with Bomber Command, a pilot."

"A pilot in Bomber Command?" Tim's dark brown eyes were shining.

"That's right," said Grandpa. "He's got some leave soon, so I told him to come here."

"Here?" Mum looked startled.

Grandpa nodded and stroked his moustache. "I told him Rose and I would be here a day or two, bringing you some pieces of furniture, bedding and things." He shook his head. "That nine pounds the government gives people who've been bombed out is ridiculous. You can't buy furniture with that!"

Grandma shook her head, frowning. "Why didn't you tell me this, George?"

"Hm. Didn't I, dear? Thought I had. Anyway, the lad only has a few days leave. Nice for him to meet our side of the family."

Tim looked across the table. Grandma was still shaking her head. Mum was staring at the tablecloth.

Grandpa looked uncomfortable. "Hrmph!" His chair scraped on the kitchen floor as he pushed it back. "I'll get the car unloaded, before the blackout, before it gets too dark and cold. Feels like snow to me."

Tim started to get up too. He winced. He hadn't really noticed his knees while he was sitting still. But now, when he tried to bend them, it felt as if the skin was held in place with hundreds of needles.

"You sit still, lad," said Grandpa. "I know you'd like to help, but I can manage. By the way, I've got some books for you."

Tim nodded glumly. He was glad about the books, but it seemed he couldn't help with anything. He hadn't kept Mum and Sarah safe. Now he couldn't even help Grandpa unload the Morris. And why were Mum and Grandma so silent?

There was a clanking of pots when Grandpa returned to the kitchen. "Brr! Bitter out there." He put the pots on the table.

Mum still said nothing. Her face was drawn, a white mask, the skin stretched tightly over her cheeks, her lips a thin, pale red line.

Grandma glared at Grandpa, shaking her head slowly. Tim looked from one to the other.

"Sorry," mumbled Grandpa. He tramped out of the kitchen, pulling the door closed behind him.

Grandma put her arm round Mum's shoulder. "You go upstairs for a while, dear. I can manage here."

Mum nodded and was just leaving as Grandpa came back. "Enid, I forgot. Here's the photograph you wanted."

Mum burst into tears and rushed out of the kitchen.

"George!" Grandma shouted, standing now with hands on hips. "You ... you insensitive, stupid — Ah! Give it to me." She held out her right hand imperiously.

"Now, what did I —"

"Not another word, George Athelstan." Grandma's voice was quiet, the words slowly spoken. "Give it to me!" She swept out of the kitchen and stomped up the stairs. Sarah, still chewing, stared after her. So did Tim.

"What did you do, Grandpa?" Tim was mystified. What was the matter with Mum?

Grandpa shook his head. "I'll not say another word, lad." He turned to the door. "I'll finish unloading." The door slammed to.

Chapter 3

The Photograph

Tim lay in bed listening to the faint hum from the light on the landing. Mum had said he could leave his door open. Grandpa had brought them a small transformer light fixture. The bulb was no bigger than the one in the torch Mum kept in her handbag, so that even if the curtains were not drawn properly, barely any light would show — certainly not enough to attract an enemy plane. But there wasn't enough light to read the book Grandpa had given him, either. It was one of Dad's favourites when he was a boy — *The Coral Island* by R. M. Ballantyne. It was about three boys stranded on an island in the South Pacific.

Tim rested his feet on the stone hot-water bottle. Grandpa George had brought that, too. It reminded Tim of the shiny old stone jugs his other grandpa, Grandpa Cecil, kept in his coal cellar. Grandpa Cecil was Mum's father. He made ginger beer. The underground cellar was the coolest place in his house.

The thought of ginger beer made Tim's mouth water. He remembered the last glass he'd had, three summers ago, the light amber liquid cool and tingling on his tongue. Grandpa Cecil still had ginger, but with rationing he couldn't get enough sugar to make the delicious drink.

Tim hadn't seen Grandpa Cecil for over a year. He'd joined the Home Guard at Eastbourne to fight the Nazis if they landed on the south coast. Mum said he was too busy to visit, but Grandma Maude was coming soon. She was a really super cook.

Tim shook his head. Thinking of the Nazis reminded him of the gas mask. His eyes were drawn to a small pipe poking out of the ceiling. It was barely visible in the faint, soft light from the hall. The end of the pipe was capped, painted white like the ceiling. All the rooms at Bramley Cottage had these gas pipes. Mum said that years ago there wasn't electricity, and houses only had gas lighting. Tim shuddered. He could imagine gas hissing out of the pipe ... and the gas mask ...

He shook his head and sat up in bed, dragging the hot-water bottle up with his feet, careful of his knees. He hated Hitler and the Nazis. Then he smiled. Sarah often got things wrong — she used to call Hitler and the Nazi Party, Hitter and the Nasty Party. Mum had said not to laugh, it was an easy mistake to make as Hitler was a horrible, nasty little man.

Tim frowned. Thinking of Sarah reminded him of something. What was it? Then he remembered. Sarah was sleeping in Mum's room so that Grandma and Grandpa could have hers. Dad's photograph was in that room. Grandma had taken it up there after Mum had run up the stairs.

Tim sighed. Mum really was acting strangely. So was Grandma. He'd wanted to see the photo, but when he'd asked Mum at supper, she got that tight-lipped look and said he could see it another day. Then Grandma said to leave Mum alone.

It wasn't fair. Dad had left for Italy at the end of last summer, and sometimes Tim found himself forgetting what he looked like. He could still feel the rough, thick khaki uniform as Dad hugged him, and he could remember the bristly, fair moustache. But Dad's face faded when he tried to think of him. Tim felt guilty. He had to look at the photograph. At Chiddingstone there'd been two photos, but they were gone now.

He rolled over, swinging his legs to the side of the bed. And winced. He'd forgotten his knees — even through his pyjamas the rough, winceyette sheets hurt the raw wounds. He sat for a while, feet dangling above the floor, waiting for the burning sensation to fade.

He shivered. Maybe Grandpa was right, maybe it would snow. Carefully, he eased himself down from the high old bed. The iron frame creaked and groaned. He waited at the door. Muffled voices filtered up from the kitchen.

Tim limped along the landing, carefully avoiding the loose floorboard. It would make a terrible noise if he stepped on it. He crept to the door of Mum's bedroom. It was slightly ajar. He gently eased it open. Faint light from the hall spilled in. There was the photograph on the dressing table, by the window.

Sarah stirred and coughed, turning onto her side. Then she sat up, opening her mouth.

"Shh!" Tim put his finger to his lips. "Quiet," he whispered.

"What are you doing?" Sarah's voice was hoarse as she whispered back. She coughed again.

Tim crossed to the dressing table and picked up the photograph. "I came to look at this. I had to."

"I've looked at it lots," said Sarah. She sniffled. "I keep forgetting what Daddy looks like."

Tim stared at his sister. He'd thought he was the only one who had trouble remembering. "You ...?" he began.

Sarah nodded. "I love Daddy. I really do, but ..."

"Come on," said Tim. "Let's take it on the landing, under the light. But mind that loose board."

As they came out of the room, Tim heard Grandpa's voice. "You have to tell them, Enid." It was loud, even through the closed door. "If you don't, then I will."

Grandma's voice was muffled and so was Mum's. It sounded as if Mum was crying. Tim looked at Sarah. What did Grandpa want Mum to tell them?

"But you can't not tell them, Enid." Grandpa's voice was raised. "It's not something you can hide, not all the time." Grandpa sounded almost angry. "And the added strain when you're expecting another baby. It's too much."

Sarah smiled at Tim. "A new baby?" She clapped her hands. "A new baby!" She jumped up and down, landing on the end of the loose board. There was a noise like a clap of thunder as the wood lifted and then slammed down.

The kitchen door burst open. Grandma stood framed in the light, her shadow stretching down the hall to the foot of the stairs. "What on earth? Children! Is that you?"

"Yes, Grandma," called Sarah.

Grandpa appeared at the door. "Did you hear all that? Did you hear what we were saying?"

"Yes, Grandpa," said Sarah. "When does Mummy get the new baby?"

"Oh, dear." Grandma breathed in deeply and shook her head. "Oh, deary me. You'd better come down."

Mum was at the kitchen table, a screwed-up handkerchief in one hand, tears streaming down her cheeks. "I'm sorry you had to hear like that," she said.

"It's all right, Mum, honest." Tim shrugged. "Did you write to Dad?"

Mum burst into tears, rocking back and forth on the kitchen chair. Grandma rushed over to her.

Grandpa sat down, shaking his head slowly, stroking his moustache. He held out his arms, beckoning to Tim and Sarah. "Come here, the two of you." He held them tightly, one on each side. "Dad doesn't know about the baby, even though Mum wrote to him. She posted the letter the day you were bombed out. With that and finding a new place, she hasn't had time to tell you. Then ..." He shook his head. "Well, Dad was reported missing in action a week ago, at a place named Anzio. Mum heard the day before yesterday. Her letter was sent back." Grandpa sighed.

Tim couldn't speak. He looked from Grandpa to Mum. Mum was nodding slowly, the tears still coming. Sarah started to cry. Grandpa tried to soothe her, and she buried her face in his cardigan, sobbing.

Grandpa sighed again and held out a piece of paper. Tim took it and read the bold, black letters across the top: POST OFFICE TELEGRAM.

It was stamped: 17FEB 44 TUNBRIDGE WELLS - KENT.

By Hand Delivery
Mrs. W.G. Athelstan
Bramley Cottage
Medbury, Nr. Tunbridge Wells

Regret to inform you that Capt. W. G. Athelstan, Corps of Royal Engineers, has been reported by his unit as believed missing. Further particulars will be forwarded as soon as received.

Under Secretary of State for War.

Tim couldn't believe it. He read the words again. Dad missing in action! Now he knew why Mum had been acting so strangely. He looked at the photograph. His hand gripped the black-painted frame so tightly that the wood bit into his palm. Dad smiled up at him, the captain's pips shining brightly on his shoulders. He remembered every detail of his father's face, as if he were there in the room.

Tim's throat ached. He couldn't breathe. It felt as if he was being pushed into dark, cold, wet earth, a thick black rubber mask pressed over his face.

Chapter 4

The Little Gentleman

It was snowing again, and Jack Frost had painted a delicate pattern over the windows during the night. Tim had hardly slept for the last two days. Was his father dead? Was he a prisoner? Was he wounded, lying on a cold, muddy battlefield, with no one nearby? Tim felt so helpless. And today he had to go to school. Sarah wasn't going. She had a cold and fever.

Grandpa George was just coming out of the bathroom. "Well, how's our young soldier today?"

"My knees are still really sore, Grandpa. My pyjamas rub on them."

"Hm. Let me have a look, lad." Grandpa led the way into the bathroom. Steam had melted the frost in the centre of the window and there was a strong smell of Lifebuoy soap. Grandpa always used Lifebuoy, even for shaving. He said that as well as making you clean, it was an antiseptic, so you got double value for your money. "Now, sit there, on the edge of the bath."

Grandpa examined the shiny, tight, reddish scabs. "Hrmph. Coming along nicely. A little Vaseline would help." He opened the medicine cabinet above the basin. "Here we are." He opened the jar and gently applied the thick yellow grease, first to the right knee and then the left. "Now, how does that feel?"

Tentatively, Tim swung first one leg and then the other. "A little better, Grandpa."

"Hrmph. Well, give it a while and I'll guarantee it'll ease up. Now, quick-smart and brush those teeth."

"Can I use your Lifebuoy soap, Grandpa?"

"On your teeth?"

"No, Grandpa," Tim laughed. "When I wash myself."

"Of course, Tim." Grandpa smiled. "But don't leave it in the water to get soft. Remember, soap's on ration, and it's difficult to get good old Lifebuoy."

Tim nodded. He remembered when soap had first been rationed. Mum had said not to wash as much. He'd gone a week without doing his neck and knees until Mum found out. And she wasn't amused when he said he was trying to save soap.

"Hurry, Tim," said Grandpa. "There's a treat for breakfast, from my secret supplier."

Tim breathed in deeply. Through the smell of Lifebuoy he thought he could smell bacon. Bacon!

Maybe there were eggs too! Where did Grandpa get his secret supplies? You could only get one egg for each person every four weeks, and bacon was rationed, too.

But when Tim asked him, Grandpa George only winked.

Tim walked, stretching his legs, trying to place his booted feet into the large footprints, now partly obscured by new snow, that led up the hill. His leather satchel banged against his side the way the cardboard box for the gas mask used to. He was pleased that he no longer had to carry the hated mask everywhere he went.

It was still snowing lightly, but the sky was brightening, the sun breaking through. His boots crunched as he plodded slowly up the hill. Grandpa thought he should stay home because there'd been such a heavy snowfall in the night, but Mum had insisted.

"School will take his mind off things, Dad. And he's missed so much lately."

Tim was glad he hadn't had to change schools when they moved to Medbury, even though it was quite a long journey on the bus to get to the convent school he went to. The school was run by nuns. When they'd moved to Chiddingstone, all the schools for older children had been full up. There was room for Sarah in the small Chiddingstone village school, but Tim had to go to the convent in Tunbridge Wells.

As he arrived at the entrance to Limekiln Farm, Tim stopped to make a snowball. A huge old conker tree grew by the gateway, its branches crystal white and gleaming in the early morning sunlight. He threw the snowball high into the tree. As it broke and fell, snow showered down. He jumped out of the way. His knees ached with cold. He wondered if Monica, the girl he had to sit next to at school, would stay home because of the bad weather. He hoped so. She smelled funny.

Tim came to the newsagents. There was liquorice root in a jar in the window. Maybe he'd get some on the way home — it was good to chew, and you could make liquorice water with it too. He'd ask Mum for the empty cod liver oil bottle. He shuddered. Cod liver oil was awful, but he and Sarah had some every day, to prevent colds. Still, it hadn't stopped Sarah getting a cold. Funny how something so awful-tasting was free, and all the nice things were rationed.

Tim ambled on past the greengrocer's and the butcher's shop. There was the triangular village green and the old Saxon church, with its square sandstone and flint tower to defend against invaders. Just beyond the lych-gate, the roofed gateway that led into the churchyard, was the bus stop. There was a large crowd there today, some people chatting and laughing, puffs of white breath disappearing, others stamping their feet, trying to keep warm. Maybe the bus wasn't running. There was no sign of Sarah's friends.

Tim ran his left hand along the top of the low stone wall by the gate. He gathered a handful of snow and packed it into a hard ball. He threw it into the churchyard, where it splattered against a tombstone.

"Oy! Show more respect for the dead." A small, thin man glared at Tim. "No respect, some kids. No manners neither." He turned. "Ah. Here's the bus."

Tim was angry. He prided himself on good manners. The bus drew into the curb, showering slushy snow onto the legs of the waiting crowd. Eyes peered out from the oval peep-holes in the brown paper covering the windows.

"Right down my boots," complained the thin man. "Now me feet are bloomin' soaking. Yargh!" He climbed onto the bus.

The bus conductor held up two fingers. "Standing room only. Two more."

The lady ahead of Tim climbed onto the bus. Tim was about to follow when he heard someone running.

"Wait for me! Wait for me!" A short, plump woman was running toward Tim, shopping bag bouncing up and down in one hand, the other waving an umbrella. "Hold it," she puffed. Then with a shriek, she slipped.

Tim jumped forward, just in time to prevent her from falling. It was almost too much for him, but somehow he managed to hold her up. His knees burned as the rough tweed of her overcoat rubbed against them.

"Thank you, young man," gasped the woman. "Proper little gentleman, you are."

"Ladies first," said Tim, ushering her onto the waiting bus. "Ladies first."

The conductor held up her hand. "Sorry, love." She rang the bell. "Have to get the next one. It won't be long."

Tim smiled as the bus pulled away. He watched it turn the corner, then ambled over to the old sandstone horse trough at the end of the churchyard wall. His feet were tingling with cold in the tight black rubber Wellington boots. His fingers, poking out from grey woollen mits, were icy too. He'd lost his new gloves in the bombing, so Grandma had made him sock-mits. Grandma never wasted anything. She cut off the worn feet from Grandpa's old socks and sewed up the rest, leaving five holes for fingers and thumb to poke through. "Make do and mend," Grandma would say, "like Mrs. Sew-and-Sew."

Tim shrugged and ran his hand through the thick snow on the horse trough. An old chestnut husk was trapped in the ice underneath, brown and battered like a miniature hedgehog. Tim made a snowball and threw it across the road, across the narrow point of the triangular village green. It hit the fence on the far side with a thud.

He aimed a second at the mark left by the first. It landed just to the right. Tim decided to make six and throw them in quick succession. He picked up the first and threw it with all his might. As he did so, a small, black car, speeding despite the snow, came roaring up the road. It was as if Tim had planned it. The driver was winding down his window to signal with his right hand. Tim watched in horror as the icy projectile hit the man's ear.

Brakes screeched. The car skidded through the snow, bumped into the curb and came to a juddering halt. Tim stood rooted to the spot. A small, fat man wrenched the door open. "Agh!" He slipped and fell, landing in the slushy snow. "Agh!" He glared at Tim.

Tim turned and vaulted the churchyard wall. He ran for his life toward the lych-gate, but the thick snow in the graveyard slowed him down.

The man was more agile than Tim had expected. He caught up with Tim as he reached the gate. Snarling, his small, beady eyes barely slits, he reached out with his leather-gloved hand. Tim ran round the stone churchyard cross. There were two headstones to his right, a table tomb to the left. He ran for the gap between them, but tripped over a flat gravestone hidden by the snow.

"Gotcha, yer little vagabond." A grasping hand gripped the collar of Tim's coat. "I'll teach yer, yer little varmint." The man lifted him up and in a single motion, stretched him flat, like a sacrifice, face down on the table tomb.

Wham! Wham! Wham! In groups of three, the man pounded Tim's behind. Wham! Wham! Wham! Again and again and again.

"Hey! What the heck!" A deep, warm voice shouted from across the green. "Hey there!"

The fat man turned and then, with a grunt, ran out of the churchyard to his car. "Young varmint," he shouted back.

"Hey there! Hold it," came the deep voice.

But the engine of the little car roared into life, and in a cloud of blue-grey smoke, the fat man was gone.

Chapter 5

Bomber Pilot

Tim climbed down from the grave. He was shaking, sobbing, as much from fright as anything else. He was cold, his trousers wet, not only from melted snow, but also from an uncontrollable disaster halfway through the beating. And his knees hurt. He looked down and saw blood.

"Hey, are you okay?"

Tim stared at the figure framed in the lychgate. Below a blue-grey, peaked cap were friendly brown eyes, and above the smiling mouth was a bristly, fair moustache. The man held a canvas kit-bag over his right shoulder. For a moment Tim thought it was his father, much younger, but his father, nevertheless, as he'd looked in one of the photographs burned and gone forever in the fire at the cottage in Chiddingstone.

"What the heck's going on?" The deep voice had a pleasant drawl. Mum would call it "that

American nasal tone." The young flying officer looked round at the trampled snow and then back at Tim. "What did that guy do to you?"

Tim continued to stare. He couldn't believe it. He knew who this was. In bold letters on the shoulders of the blue-grey airforce uniform was the word CANADA. He sniffled and then wiped his nose with the back of his mitt. "Are you Bill?" he said. "Bill, from Canada?" And before the startled pilot could reply — "You're Bill Brewer, aren't you?"

"Well, would you believe it? Are you Enid's boy?"

Tim nodded. "We thought you were coming yesterday, or the day before."

The Canadian pilot breathed in deeply and pursed his lips. "I was," he said. "Got sort of side-tracked in London with some of the boys." He looked down at Tim. "Gee, don't tell me you guys have been coming to wait for me. Have you?"

Tim smiled. "No. I was going to school, but the bus was full. Then I threw this snowball. I didn't mean to hit him, but it went in his window, and ..."

Bill was laughing. "Did it hit him?" he asked, half-spluttering.

Tim nodded. "But ... why are you laughing?"

Bill was now roaring with laughter. It was a rich, full-throated, infectious laugh and soon Tim joined in. He couldn't help himself.

Bill wiped his eyes with his free hand. "Same sort of thing happened to me when I was your age. We were having one heck of a snow fight one day, in the school yard. Chuck Matthews had just hit me and knocked my toque off."

Tim wondered what a toque was. Maybe it was a Canadian way of saying "knock your head off," or "knock your block off." Mum didn't like him saying things like that.

Bill was continuing. "I threw a snowball at Chuck, but he ducked, just as the vice-principal was coming out of the side door. It hit him right in the ... Well, it doesn't matter. But did I ever get a beating. Nobody would believe me when I said it was an accident." He looked down at Tim.

"Did you get the cane?" asked Tim. The vice-principal sounded a rather important kind of person. Maybe he was like a headmaster?

Bill shook his head. "No. The strap. Old Inckman had a thick belt, which he kept in his office." He shrugged and looked at Tim. "Couldn't help remembering that. Seeing that man hitting you, and then all this snow, reminds me of home." He sighed deeply, looking round. Then he turned back to Tim. "Are you okay?"

Tim nodded. His behind did hurt. The man had really pummelled him. But he didn't want Bill to think he wasn't brave. "I'm just wet," he said.

There was the whine of an engine as the dark-green Maidstone and District bus appeared out of the trees beyond the churchyard. Tim turned and watched as it slowed to a crawl. There was no one waiting at the stop. The bus drove slowly by and then, as the driver changed gears, picked up speed and was soon out of sight. The snow began to fall in heavier, softer flakes. Tim picked up his satchel full of books from beside the table tomb. His knees were really hurting.

Bill looked at him. "Your bus?"

Tim nodded. "But I can't go to school like —"

"No, you — Say, I don't even know your name."

"Tim. Tim Athelstan."

The Canadian officer laughed, quietly this time, a deep rumbling sound. "I know the Athelstan bit. It was your first name I didn't know." He held out his right hand. "Hi there, Tim. Good to know you."

Tim solemnly shook hands. "How do you do, sir?"

"Ha!" Bill roared with laughter. "You don't have to call me sir. You just call me Bill, like you did just now. Okay?"

Tim nodded. "Okay ... Bill." He wouldn't say okay in front of Mum — she called it slang. But he wondered what she'd say when Bill used it.

"Now, how far is it to your house?" Bill removed his hand from where it had been resting on Tim's shoulder and hoisted his kit-bag onto his own shoulder.

"It's not far," said Tim. "Down the hill."

Bill smiled. "Good. When I spoke to Uncle George last week, he said you'd had to move.

Lucky I phoned ahead, right? Devil's own job getting hold of Uncle, though. The phone system's not like the one in Canada."

Tim turned sharply away. He didn't want Bill to see the tears beginning to well up, threatening to spill down his cheeks. Every time he thought of leaving Chiddingstone, he thought of Dad. That's where Dad would think they were. If he was alive, he'd remember the old Kentish cottage with the red tile roof and tile-hung walls. Dad loved old things. He said they were the heart-blood of England. And the Nazis were destroying everything.

"Hey, what's up? You're not hurt are you? Those knees look painful."

Tim shook his head. "No. I'm all right." He took a deep breath. "But before we get home, you'd better know about Dad."

Bill squatted down and lowered his kit-bag into the thick snow. He turned Tim to face him and rested both hands on Tim's shoulders. "Now, tell me. What about your dad?"

"He's missing." The words stuck in Tim's throat. "Missing in action at Anzio." He hissed out the words.

"Bloody war." Bill shook his head and breathed in deeply, looking up at the falling snow. "Bloody war."

Chapter 6

Bill Brewer

"You've no idea who it was, Tim?"

Tim shook his head. "No, Mum. I've never seen him before. He was just a man. A short, fat man with squinty, beady eyes." He shuddered. "I couldn't see much of his face because of his hat and scarf."

Bill shook his head. "Took off before I got there. Wish I'd arrived sooner."

"How did you get there?" asked Grandpa. "The bus to Goudhurst doesn't run that early."

"Hitched a ride, Uncle," said Bill. He yawned. "I'd come down to Tunbridge Wells from London on the milk train ... I think that's what they called it."

Grandpa nodded. "That's right."

Bill laughed. "Have to be careful what I say, sometimes. You have funny names for things here."

"You cheeky monkey," said Grandma. "Talk about funny names for things — what about you Canadians?"

"Now, now, Rose." Grandpa frowned. "Don't get into that."

Grandma smiled. "Only joking, George. You should know me better after all these years."

"What's toque mean, Bill?" asked Tim.

"Toque?" Bill shrugged. "It's a wool hat you wear in winter. Don't you have them?"

"Never heard of it," said Grandma. "Now, if you'd said balaclava I'd know what you meant."

Bill shook his head. "It's not quite like that, Aunt Rose. It doesn't pull down with a hole for your face."

Grandpa shook his head. "Hrmph. Weren't you telling us how you got here, Bill?"

Bill grinned. "Was I? Oh, yes. Anyway, I arrived at about five-thirty this morning. Talk about a slow train! It seemed to stop at every little place on the way. I didn't sleep for fear of missing the station. Anyway, I asked for directions, then started walking. A bit confusing with all the road signs gone."

Tim nodded. It was confusing. But, with the threat of invasion four years ago, all the signs had been removed. If enemy troops did land, they'd find it difficult to find out where they were, even if they had maps.

"You walked?" said Mum. "All the way here?"

Bill shook his head. "Not all the way. I hitched a ride for the last part. Not far mind you, but it did get me there in time to see that guy beating on Tim."

"Oh, I wish I knew who it was." Mum's lips formed a thin hard line. "Just look at this coat — torn, and I don't have enough coupons for another. It was the best utility I could get. When I think of all the things burned at Chiddingstone, and —"

"Calm down, dear, I'm sure I can fix it." Grandma took the coat. She nodded. "Leave it to me. It will take time, but it's something I can do whilst I'm here."

"Thanks, Mum." Tim's mother sighed. "I'm so strung up these days. And thank you too, Bill. Oh dear, what a greeting for you." She turned to Tim. "Now, upstairs, young man, and off with those sopping wet clothes or you'll catch your death of cold." She shook her head. "Maybe you should have stayed at home, after all."

Tim tried to run up the stairs, but the new bandages Grandma had put on his knees were too tight. He didn't want to miss anything. Bill was only staying for the day. He had to return to base in the evening.

"I'll sure be glad when this tour's over," Bill was saying, as Tim came into the kitchen.

"We'll all be glad when the war's over," said Grandma. "But what's wrong with this tour, Bill?"

Bill had his hands on his lap, hidden by the table. But, as Tim approached from the kitchen door, he could see the left one shaking. Bill obviously noticed it too because he quickly placed his right hand over the left. Tim could see the knuckles whiten. Bill laughed, a short, high-pitched, jerky sound, not the deep rumble Tim had already grown used to. He shrugged. "Nothing, I guess. Much the same as the last one. This is my second, you know."

Grandpa shook his head. "Your second tour?"

"Yes. The boys and I flew Darling D-for-Daisy until a few months back — a wizard old Halifax bomber. Then we switched to Lancasters."

"You fly a Lancaster?" Tim almost shouted. That would be something to tell his friends — Binky here in Medbury, and John and his other pals at the convent school.

Bill was nodding absently. "Sparks hated the switch — still does. He almost refused to fly. He's getting another pigeon."

Tim wondered if everyone else was as confused as he was with this talk of sparks and pigeons.

"Hrmph," said Grandpa. "Hrmph! I'm not sure I understand, Bill. This Sparks of yours ..."

"We call him Sparks because he's the radio operator."

"Yes, I know that." Grandpa nodded. "Wireless operators are often nicknamed Sparks. It's the pigeon I'm not sure about."

"Oh. Sorry." Bill smiled. "You see, in the old

Halifax and Wellington bombers we always carried a pigeon. If we were shot down, then it was Sparks's job to write our position, the map coordinates, on a slip of paper and put it in the message container on the bird's leg."

"I see," said Mum. "The bird would fly home, and at the base they'd know where to look for you."

"That's right." Bill smiled. "We never had to use Oscar — that's what Sparks called the bird. He grew really attached to it. He called it our mascot, and it was, in a way. Sparks is superstitious. He had a ritual. He would walk round our plane, old Darling D-for-Daisy, three times, talking to Oscar before we took off. Sometimes I'd grab him and try to get him into the old kite after only two goes round. It was no good. 'Three's lucky,' Sparks always said."

"So, why don't you have a pigeon now?" asked Sarah. It was the question Tim had been dying to ask. He glared across at his sister. She frowned back.

Bill ruffled her long fair hair. "They tell us we don't need them. In the Lancaster we have a hand-cranked radio transmitter instead."

"Surely that's better, isn't it, Bill?"

Bill looked across at Grandma. "Not really, Aunt Rose. They're heavy and cumbersome. All the guys I know hate them. They'd much rather have a pigeon."

"But why?"

"I guess it's partly superstition. You get into a sort of routine — Sparks walking three times round the plane, things like that. When something breaks the pattern, it affects you, especially if it's taken away, bang, just like that."

Tim noticed that when Bill said "bang" his left hand started to shake again. Hurriedly, Bill clamped his right hand over the left.

"Sparks asked me if it would be okay to get another pigeon. I told him it was fine with me. He won't be able to have it in a loft on the field, like we had at the old Halifax base," Bill went on, "but he says he's located some pigeon fanciers near the new field and they're going to arrange something between them." He looked round the table. Everyone was quiet. "Sorry if I've been boring you."

"Oh, no, dear," said Grandma. "We think we have a hard time, but you young men, day in and day out ..."

"Well, it's not actually every day," said Bill. "But, say, I meant to tell you. I bet I've flown over here a few times."

"Over here?" said Tim.

"Close, I bet." Bill nodded excitedly. "You see, suppose we're raiding somewhere like Dormstadt. We fly south over Reading, to avoid London. Don't want to get shot down before we get going."

"Shot down? Over London!" Grandma's face was a picture.

Bill laughed. "There's so much flak round London that we avoid it, to be on the safe side." He chuckled. "Anyway, then we fly over this way, Tunbridge Wells area, and then on down to Beachy Head and set our course for the target."

"I know Beachy Head," said Tim excitedly. "When we go to visit Uncle Ray and Aunt Sue, at Eastbourne, Uncle takes me and Dad prawning on the rocks. You remember, Mum?"

Tim looked at Mum. Her head was bowed, and he could see a handkerchief screwed up in the hand held up to her face. Her shoulders were shaking. He looked at Grandma and then back at Mum. "I didn't mean ..."

Grandma nodded and stood up, resting her hand on Mum's shoulder. "No more talk. You men go out and fetch some wood. We'll think about something to fill your stomachs. Did you say something about Granger's Wood, Enid?"

Mum nodded and dabbed at her eyes. She looked up, a forced smile on her lips. "That's right, Mum. They're clearing an area down there." Her voice was barely above a whisper. "We walked there on Sunday, Tim, remember?" She dabbed at her tear-stained cheeks.

"I'll find it, Mum," said Tim quietly. "Where's the chopper?"

"By the side of the coal-bin."

"Why is it just men who get to go out?" said Sarah. "Why can't I go?" She sniffed.

"Because, young lady, you have a bad cold." Grandma pushed her firmly back into her seat. "You sit there and we'll find you something to do."

Sarah scowled.

"Do you have a superstition, Bill?" asked Tim as they walked down the hill.

Bill shrugged. "I have my dime. I huff on it and give it a quick polish before we scramble. I'll not leave that behind."

"What's a dime?" said Tim.

"Here, I'll show you." Bill reached into the left breast pocket of his tunic and carefully pulled out a neatly folded handkerchief. As he unfolded it, Tim saw that one of the corners had been sewn in to form a miniature pocket. From this, Bill took out a tiny silver coin.

"That's a silver threepenny piece," said Tim.

Bill shook his head. "Same size maybe, same colour, but it's a dime — ten cents, Canadian. Now, see the date?"

Tim saw the date — 1920 — printed beneath a wreath. And he read the words CANADA and TEN CENTS. Bill turned over the coin. There was the head of King George V.

"I was born in nineteen-twenty," said Bill. "I got this on my tenth birthday and I kept it in my room until I joined the airforce. Now it's my lucky charm." He carefully pushed it back into the special pocket and folded the handkerchief. "Always with me. I don't let Sciver see that."

"Who's Sciver?" asked Grandpa George.

"He's an L.A.C. at the new base," said Bill. "A lazy, good-for-nothing leading aircraftsman in the parachute store. Mind you, I call him lazy, but he's got to be strong to heave those parachutes around the way he does. When we go out on a mission, we have to leave all our personal belongings in the store when we pick up our parachutes and escape packs. He's a miserable son — Well, he's got a cushy job, but never a smile, never a cheery word. Just looks you up and down with those bleak, mean, empty eyes as if he's measuring you for a coffin. Horrible little man."

Tim shuddered. This Sciver sounded nasty.

"Not the kind of person to make you feel good before a dangerous trip," said Grandpa.

"That's for sure," said Bill. "And there's talk that he gets extra meals, meant for the aircrews. He's fat enough, the little blighter."

"We're here," said Tim suddenly. "This is the place Mum meant."

"But where's the wood?" asked Bill.

"There," said Tim. "Those trees they've chopped down."

"Those?" Bill burst out laughing, that rich, rumbling sound. "That's the wood? I thought we were going to fell a good-sized tree and buck it and split it. Mind you, I was wondering how we were going to do it with that meat cleaver you have there."

"It's not a meat cleaver, it's a chopper," said Tim. And he hacked angrily at one of the fallen branches strewn on the woodland floor.

Chapter 7

The Wireless

"I didn't mean to be rude, Bill," said Tim. He was thinking about the meat chopper incident.

"I know, Tim. It's funny, isn't it? Here are you and me talking the same language, yet sometimes I'll say something you don't get and another time, you'll use a word that I find strange."

Tim nodded. They were standing outside the newsagent's shop while Grandpa bought some tobacco and a newspaper.

Bill looked up at the sky. "That old moon up there will be shining over home in a few hours." He sighed. "Real bomber's moon, that one."

"Bomber's moon? What do you mean, Bill?" Tim looked up at the round silver ball.

Bill shifted his kit-bag on his shoulder. "Well, it's nice and bright — makes it easy to see the target or to spot landmarks. But it's not too high, and there's enough cloud to cover it occasionally, so we can slip in without being seen."

Tim thought he knew what Bill meant. But another thought was nagging him. "Do you like bombing people, Bill?"

Bill shook his head. "I try not to think about it. I'm given a target, a bomb factory, a submarine dock, a power plant. It's my job to get there safely, drop our load and get us back to base in one piece. And I sure as hell don't want That Man getting over here, or anywhere."

"Neither do I," said Tim. "But Grandpa says we'll stop him. Grandpa says Hitler's lost his chance now. And Tommy Handley says so, too."

"Hey! Do you listen to ITMA, Tommy Handley and the crew? On the radio?" Bill chuckled. "It's a great show, isn't it? That Mrs. Mopp and Colonel Chinstrap, and Mona Lott and Ali-Oop. Great stuff! Sparks loves it."

"I don't get to hear it much," said Tim. "Mum doesn't let me listen to the wireless that late. And since I lost my tin mug in the bombing, I haven't heard it at all."

"Tin mug?" said Bill. "Is that some kind of English radio or something?"

Tim burst out laughing. He couldn't help it. He doubled up and roared till his cheeks hurt.

"Did I say something funny?" asked Bill.

Tim caught his breath. "It's just a tin mug, Bill. It's a cup that you drink out of."

"Oh, a tin mug, like for camping."

Tim nodded. "But I used mine to listen to the wireless. I'd turn it upside down on the floor and put my ear on the bottom of it. The sound came through quite well. I couldn't hear everything though, especially if Mum was laughing, or Grandma and Grandpa were visiting and they were talking, but —"

"Now, what were Grandma and Grandpa talking about?" Grandpa came out of the shop. Warm air, full of interesting smells, flowed out after him.

"Tim was telling me how he listens to ITMA," said Bill.

"Really." Grandpa nodded. "So, you listen to Tommy Handley and the gang? Thought your mother packed you off to bed before that."

"She does," said Tim quietly. Now he was going to be found out.

"He listens through a tin mug," said Bill. "On the floor. The vibrations carry the voices."

Grandpa started to chuckle. "You clever young blighter." He patted Tim on the back. "That's a good one. Never have been able understand why you aren't allowed to listen. It's all good fun. Good for morale."

"Does that mean you won't tell Mum?" asked Tim. In the moonlight he could see Grandpa wink at Bill.

"Let's call it our secret, shall we? Just the three of us." Grandpa chuckled. "Tin mug. I'll be damned."

Bill had been standing silently, listening. "I've got an idea," he said. "Next time I visit, I'll make you a crystal set. I'm sure Sparks can get me the parts. I know he's got a spare headset around somewhere."

"Headset?" said Grandpa.

"Earphones," said Bill, laughing. "On a clear night you'll get great reception, Tim. You may even pick up a channel or two from France or Holland. They're not too far. But, for sure, you'll get ITMA loud and clear."

"You mean, you'll make me a wireless?" said Tim.

"Yep." Bill grinned. "Made one or two when I was younger. You see, a crystal set doesn't need electricity. And with your earphones," he winked at Grandpa, "you'll feel just like a radio operator up there in a big old L-for-Lucky Lancaster."

Tim couldn't believe it. Then, in the distance he heard the whine of an engine slowing down. "It's the bus! It's coming!" he cried out. "Hurry! The bus is coming."

The two men followed as Tim ran, half hobbling, toward the bus stop. Coming through the trees were pin-pricks of light, barely visible. Tim slid along the hard-packed snow, coming to a stop at the lych-gate. They were just in time.

"Lucky you heard that, Tim. Thanks." Bill was a little puffed. "If I'd missed this bus, I'd've missed the train and been AWOL at base."

The pin-pricks of light grew larger, light piercing the darkness from the covers on the headlights of the bus — on one side a tiny beam, the size of a penny; on the other, horizontal bands of light slanting downwards. The brown paper-covered windows, with their small, oval peep-holes, slid by as the bus drew to a halt.

"Hi, there, Canada," said the lady conductor. "Coming with me, are you?"

Bill laughed.

The clippie winked at Tim and then at Grandpa. "Come on then. Hop on. You can be my valentine."

Bill grasped the handrail and heaved himself aboard. "Is it Valentine's Day?"

"Tomorrow, luv. And remember, it's a leap-year. You'd better watch out." She rang the bell. "Hold on tight."

"'Bye, Tim," called Bill, laughing. "Remember, you'll be L-for-Lucky Lancaster next time. 'Bye, Uncle."

They stood waving, Tim half excited, half scared. Bill looked so like Dad.

Grandpa sighed and shook his head. "That boy is a real Athelstan. That fair straight hair and dark brown eyes. Good square shoulders too."

"Does he remind you of Dad, Grandpa?"

Grandpa George nodded slowly. "He does, Tim. As soon as I saw him, I could see my sister Ruby. But you're right. He reminds me of your father a few years back."

"Is Dad going to come home?" Tim's voice was a whisper. There was silence. Tim looked up at Grandpa. The old man had his eyes closed, head tilted up, as if praying, the moonlight highlighting every line on his face.

"God willing, son. God willing." Then he breathed in deeply, took Tim's hand in his own, and set off down the path. "If we hurry, we'll catch the six o'clock news. Come on, lad."

> *"This is the BBC Home Service. Here is the six o'clock news, read by Freddie Grisewood.*
>
> *This morning General Alexander arrived at the beachhead at Anzio. He toured the front, talking to the commanders and spending considerable time with the troops. Following his visit, he called a press conference and assured correspondents that there was not going to be any Dunkirk at Anzio.*
>
> *He had high praise for all our brave fighting men, but in particular he mentioned the courage of the Fifty-sixth Division — the London Division, men who have been embroiled in the bitter fighting for the past several months and who again gave of themselves unstintingly. He —"*

Grandma leaned forward and clicked off the wireless.

Mum was quietly sobbing. "I'm going *upstairs*

for a while," she said. "You keep it on, if you want. I know Dad likes to listen to the news."

"Do you need company, Enid?"

Mum shook her head. "Thanks, Mum. I'd rather be by myself at the moment."

Chapter 8

Chalky White

After school, Tim dawdled along behind the group of girls ahead. Sarah was chatting with some of her friends. They were laughing, marching in an exaggerated goose-step.

"Heil Hitler! Yah, yah, yah!
What a silly man you are,
With your black moustache and hair like tar!
Heil Hitler! Yah, yah, yah!"

Sarah was lucky. Medbury wasn't far from Chiddingstone, and some of Sarah's friends lived in the village. None of Tim's school chums did. Tim shrugged and hobbled along, one foot in the gutter, one on the curb.

The snow was almost gone, melting in the late February sunshine. But where the sun could not reach, snow lingered, icy, crystalline patches that crunched underfoot. Tim looked up at the trees on the other side of the board fence. They looked like chestnuts. He'd have to ask Binky.

And he'd have to ask Binky if he'd heard ITMA last night. Tim had tried to listen. He'd had a brainwave — if a tin mug worked then so should an empty tin. Tim was washing up at the time. They'd had Spam for dinner. He washed and dried the Spam tin and hid it in his trouser pocket. The small, black tabletop wireless was in the kitchen. Tim's room was at the front of the house, on the opposite side. He'd only been able to make out the beginning of the show:

"It's that man again, it's that man again,
Mr. Tommy Handley is here."

What Tommy said next was a jumble. Tim pressed his ear to the metal, but the narrow, oblong base of the tin was uncomfortable. He opened the bedroom door wide, but Mum had the kitchen door shut. All he could hear were muted voices. Then he had another brainwave. The bathroom was over the kitchen. He crept along the hall. Lying down on the lino in the bathroom, he was just in time to hear that Mr. Handley had changed his farm into a big air base. It was cold lying on the bathroom floor. He should have put on his dressing gown. He shivered. He wondered if Bill was listening.

The kitchen door opened. "Is that you, Tim?"

"I'm going to the toilet, Mum."

"Well, remember to pull the chain, dear."

"I will, Mum."

Sarah came into the bathroom, rubbing her eyes.

"What are you doing in here on the floor, Tim?"

Tim got up, hiding the tin behind his back.

"Mummy said to pull the chain. You always forget."

Tim sighed. He flushed the toilet. The cistern hissed and gurgled. Tim shuffled back to his room. Just wait till he had that crystal set!

Thinking of the night before reminded Tim that, today, Grandpa was getting the men to bring the new bomb shelter. It wasn't going to be an Anderson, dug into the back garden, with a curved, corrugated iron roof covered with earth and thick sods of grass. This one was a Morrison, a small shelter that was put right in the house. His school friend John, who lived with his grand-parents above a pub at Faridge, said they had a Morrison down in the cellar. It was made of iron, like a huge table, with the thick, steel top bolted to heavy metal legs. The sides were metal grill. Tim wondered where Mum would put theirs. Not near a window, he was sure. She'd told him that people had had their throats cut from glass flying through the grill.

Tim was so deep in thought that he stumbled into a group of girls standing at the corner. Two of them lived down the lane beyond Limekiln Farm. They were older than the others. They giggled.

One leaned over and kissed Tim on his cheek. Her lips were wet. "Will you marry me, Tim?"

The others started to laugh. Tim blushed and wiped his cheek with his mitt. He was fed up with all this kissing. Ever since Valentine's Day, the girls had been teasing him. Now he knew what the clippie had meant by it being a leap year — it meant the girls could ask the boys to marry them. And it wasn't finished yet. February the twenty-ninth was still to come. It was stupid. He hated it.

"Yah, yah! Look who likes to play with girls!"

The girls stopped giggling. Tim whirled round and saw Chalky White, a boy who lived on his road. Chalky had started to taunt Tim as soon as the Athelstans moved in two weeks ago. He mocked the children who wore the dark blue serge uniform of the convent school. He called them Mussolini's toadies because they went to a Catholic school and because the Pope lived in Italy. Binky said to watch out for Chalky. He was a bully. He always picked on children smaller than he was, and he didn't fight unless he had a gang with him.

Tim looked at the grinning faces of the boys with Chalky. They were all bigger than Tim. Where was Binky? He should have been on the later bus with Chalky, and got off when Chalky did.

"Yah! Scaredy!" shouted Chalky.

Tim was furious. He wasn't Catholic. And anyway, John and the other children at the convent who *were* hated Hitler and Mussolini as much as he did. So did the nuns. And Dad was missing, fighting Hitler's Nazis in Italy, while Chalky's dad wasn't even in the forces.

"Mussolini's friend," taunted Chalky, in a sing-song voice. "Mussolini's friend."

Tim screamed and charged.

The force of Tim's attack obviously took Chalky by surprise. The older boy was thrown to the ground, and Tim got in a few good blows before the other boys realized that their leader was in trouble.

"Help me!" shouted Chalky.

The boys dragged Tim off their friend and held him. He kicked and struggled as Chalky scrambled up from the ground. Chalky's face was red, screwed up in fury, his breathing short and rapid. He pulled back his arm to hit Tim.

Sarah screamed and ran at Chalky. She grabbed his arm. "Leave my brother alone." The boy snarled and pushed her away. She fell to the ground, losing her satchel. One of the boys grabbed it.

Tim got one arm free. His cap fell off. He flailed around, and the boy holding his other arm ducked and let go. Sarah was getting up. Tim ran over and pushed her behind him, back against the fence. As he did so, he felt a blow on the side of his head. Then he faced the crowd.

Chalky drew his arm back again, smiling now.

"Chalky!" It was Binky. "Chalky!"

Tim saw the bigger boy's smile disappearing as he turned.

"Leave him alone, Chalky." Binky's voice was low and quiet. "He's my friend."

"Yah! So what?" Chalky looked round. His own gang was dispersing, edging round the crowd.

"So, leave him alone," said Binky, again very quietly.

Chalky looked round once more. There was no one to support him. He glared at Tim, then bellowed and rushed at Binky and his friends, pushing his way through before they realized what was happening. Two turned to give chase.

"He's not worth it," said Binky. "Let him go." He smiled at Tim. "Are you all right?"

Tim nodded. "But I lost my cap."

One of the girls came forward. She held out a crumpled blue peaked cap. "Here it is, Tim."

Tim sighed with relief. "Thank you. My mum would have been furious." He turned to Sarah. "Thanks for trying to fight Chalky, Sarah."

Sarah shrugged. "I don't like him," she said. She picked up her satchel from where the boy had dropped it. "I'm going to tell Mummy."

Binky wandered up. "You don't have to worry about him. He'll be careful now he knows you're my friend. He's just mean because of his dad."

"What do you mean?" asked Tim.

"His dad can't get in the forces," said Binky. "He's got some kind of illness."

"Like a disease?" asked Tim.

Binky laughed. "I hadn't thought of it like

that." He shrugged. "He's just sick." He looked at Tim. "Do you want to be with us?"

Tim looked at the other boys. He nodded.

"Right," said Binky. "You'll have to learn to speak our language."

"Pidass thiddy sidalt plidease, Sidarah."

Everyone sitting round the Morrison eating supper looked at Tim.

"What on earth are you talking about?" said Mum.

"Nidothing, Midum." Tim grinned. "Nothing, Mum."

"He's talking that secret language Binky and the other boys use," said Sarah. "He won't tell me what it is."

"Well, it wouldn't be secret if everyone knew it," Tim replied. "Would you pass the salt please, Sarah?"

And so it had gone all evening, Tim trying a few phrases and everyone looking at him.

Mum had decided to put the Morrison in the kitchen. The kitchen was large, almost the size of two rooms, so there was plenty of space. And Mum said they'd be cosier there, as it was always warm. Tim liked the idea. They could listen to the wireless. Maybe they'd have to use the shelter when ITMA was on.

Now he lay in bed, quietly practising his secret language. It was easy really. All you had to do was add ID to the first part of a word and it sounded like double-Dutch. To stop people learning what you were doing, Binky changed the letters every day. Tomorrow it was OP.

"ChOPalky WhOPite OPis OPa fOPool," said Tim under his breath. "SOPilly OPold ChOPalky."

Tim smiled in the dark. Binky would be pleased. And tomorrow was Friday — he'd be able to go up to the back field on Saturday afternoon. Perhaps Binky would let him have a turn with the parachute. Some of the others had parachutes, but not like Binky's. One of the boys had made one from a polkadot handkerchief. It was small, and no good for running and jumping, but it was the best for rolling up and throwing. It went really high before floating gently down to the ground.

Tim rolled over onto his side. Next time Bill was down, he'd ask him about parachutes. Maybe the RCAF had flare parachutes like Binky's. He snuggled into the pillow, then raised his head. What was that? It was the drone of distant aircraft. He waited. Would the siren wail? Binky said they hadn't had an alert in Medbury for some time now.

The drone of engines grew louder. Tim climbed out of bed and shut his bedroom door. He drew back the heavy curtains, ducking under the blackout cloth that covered the window. The night sky was dotted with stars. The sound of the planes was becoming stronger, sending vibrations through the house, through the floor and up through Tim's feet and legs. He peered up at the sky. Nothing. Then he saw them, cross-shaped black shadows against the starry backdrop, huge wings stretching out, each wing with two engines thrusting forward through the night, south to the coast. They had to be Lancasters. One of them had to be Bill! Tim waved. The vibrations lessened and the hum began to fade.

Tim waited by the window in case there were more. He hadn't been able to count them. Sometimes they came in two or three waves. But all was silent now. He ducked back under the blackout cloth, shut the curtains and climbed back into bed. The old frame creaked and groaned. Where were the Lancasters going? They wouldn't all come back. He'd heard Bill tell Grandpa that a lot of planes were lost, especially the ones with new aircrews. Well, Bill wasn't new. This was his second tour. But Tim remembered Bill's hand shaking. He wondered if Sparks had the new pigeon.

Chapter 9

The Letter

"Hurry up now, Tim, Grandma's waiting."

"Coming, Mum."

Grandma Maude, his mother's mum, had arrived the last week in March.

"Sorry I couldn't get here earlier, Enid," she'd said. "You know Dad — always wants his meals on time. Never known a man who likes his food so much."

Tim didn't blame Grandpa Cecil for liking his food. Grandma Maude was the best cook he knew, even better than Mum, and Mum was jolly good. Somehow, Grandma could make the most uninteresting things taste delicious. Mum said it was the seasoning Grandma used. Last night they'd had bacon roly-poly, with gravy. Grandma had a knack of persuading butchers and grocers, even if she didn't know them, to spare that extra something, off-ration. She'd got bacon bits yesterday and a piece of suet. Tim could still taste the crumbly slices of hot, savoury roly-poly. He wondered what Grandma would manage today. She was walking them to the bus stop that morning, to be at the butcher's early.

"That's a nice scarf, Mum."

"You must have seen it before, Enid. It's an old one. I've had it for years." Grandma tied the faded polkadot scarf under her chin. "There. Lovely feeling, silk. Come along, you two."

Sarah took hold of Grandma's hand. "I'm ready, Grandma."

Grandma smiled. "Good girl." She looked round. "Now, where is that boy? Tim!"

"Here, Grandma." Tim appeared from the kitchen. "I'd forgotten my sandwiches." He pushed the waxed paper package into his satchel, careful not to squeeze too hard. Mum had made two sweetened condensed milk sandwiches as a treat today. The condensed milk was something Grandma had bought, off-ration, at the grocer's.

After school, Tim hung his satchel on the newel post at the foot of the stairs. Then he took off his cap and coat. As he hung them up, his hand brushed against the old silk scarf. It had a soft, smooth feel.

"Tea's on the table!"

There was bread and margarine, thinly spread by Grandma's expert hand. And while shopping, Grandma had found some Marmite. Tim loved the sharp, strong, tangy taste of the dark spread. He took a mouthful of tea before swallowing the bread. It was good, the way the hot liquid mingled with the sharp taste of the Marmite.

"Swallow one mouthful before taking another," said Grandma.

"Yes, Grandma." Tim took another bite of bread and Marmite. "Can I look at the paper, Mum?"

"You may, Tim." His mother nodded. "But first I want to tell you something."

There was a tone in his mother's voice that made Tim stop before taking another bite.

"I had a letter from the army today."

Tim's dark brown eyes widened. They'd discussed the possibilities — if Dad was dead, someone would visit the house. If he was a prisoner of war, the Red Cross would notify them by letter. "Dad's a prisoner," he said. But then he remembered, Mum had said the letter came from the army.

Mum pursed her lips and shook her head. "We don't know, Tim. He might be, but the Red Cross hasn't been informed. This letter is from Daddy's commanding officer." Mum held up a buff-coloured envelope. On it were the letters OHMS. That meant On His Majesty's Service. "I'll let you read it later," said Mum. "But he says how brave Daddy was the day he went missing. They were under very heavy fire, Daddy and Sergeant Morse, clearing mines for the infantry. They're both missing. Daddy was mentioned in dispatches."

Tim could feel his chest swelling, his heart beating almost to bursting. Being mentioned in dispatches was almost like getting a medal. Then he felt tears stinging the corners of his eyes. He sniffed and blinked quickly, several times, forcing the tears back.

"The main thing is ..." Mum looked across the Morrison, "after the battle and since, they've carefully searched and identified the men who ..." She paused. "They haven't found Daddy. There's a good chance he's a prisoner, perhaps in hospital, and we'll hear. Or maybe he's hiding somewhere."

Tim told Binky and the others the next day.

"That's good, Tim," said Binky. "I bet he's not a prisoner. I bet he's hiding somewhere, trying to get back. That's what my dad would do."

Tim nodded. Bill had said it was every man's duty to try and escape. He wondered if they had escape packs in the army, like Bill had. Bill had told him about the special buttons on his battle-dress that unscrewed and were a compass. They had foreign money, too, and a map of Europe printed on silk. The bit that had interested Tim most, apart from the compass, was the food — hard candy, Bill called it, and chocolate.

"Come on," said Binky in secret code. "Let's bail out. Scramble!"

The small group of boys ran up the road, arms stretched out on either side, each making his own version of the sound of a plane's engine. Tim's lips were tingling by the time they reached the back field.

"Here, Tim. Have a go." Binky held out his parachute. Binky hadn't even had a go himself! "Go on."

Tim took the parachute and scrambled up onto the potato mound. It was a bit taller than he was, and stretched halfway down the field. The sods of grass that covered it were just beginning to grow.

"They're going to move these next week," said Binky. "My mum heard from Mr. Pearson." Mr. Pearson was the air raid warden. He lived two doors down from Tim. "They won't build another one until they harvest the new crop, so we'd better make the best of it."

Tim scrambled up the end of the mound. The breeze played through his fair hair, and he breathed in deeply. He ran for the far end and jumped as high as he could. The 'chute opened above his head with a slight tug. He hit the ground and rolled over.

"Good one, Tim. This breeze is just right." Binky held out his hand.

"I wish I had a parachute," said Tim.

"Well, get some cloth and we'll make one." Binky turned to the group. "Let's throw them. It's a wizard wind." He rolled up his parachute and wrapped the strings round it. The other boys did the same to their 'chutes. They climbed onto the mound. "You give the command, Tim."

"Ready?" shouted Tim. "Steady? Go!"

Five balls shot into the air above the back field. One by one, the 'chutes opened, floating to the ground. The last was small, and covered in polkadots. Tim looked at it thoughtfully.

"This is really good material for a parachute, Tim. It's silk." Tim and Binky were seated behind the potato mound. "Do you have the string?"

Tim handed him a small ball of twine. Binky cut four pieces of equal length, measuring from his chin to the end of his outstretched arm. His penknife was not very sharp, and the ends of the twine were frayed. But when he made a clove-hitch and attached the first end of the string to one corner of the scarf, the frayed end didn't show. Soon all the strings were attached, and Binky knotted the loose ends together. He dug deep into his pocket and brought out a heavy steel nut. He attached this.

"Right. Let's try it. Scramble!"

They stood on the potato mound. Tim gave a mighty throw and the new 'chute soared into the air and opened.

"Smashing!" said Binky. "Simply smashing! That's a really wizard parachute, Tim."

Tim grinned. "Thanks, Binky." The parachute floated slowly down to earth, and as the nut touched the ground, the old silk folded gently onto the grass.

Later that day, six parachutes floated down together. Two were polkadot, one larger than the other.

A few days later there were only five again.

"Did you hear about Freddy?" asked Binky.

"No. What happened."

"He broke his leg." Binky shook his head. "Jumped out of his window."

"Jumped out of his window?"

"He thought his parachute would break his fall," said Binky. "He has to have his leg in a plaster of Paris cast for weeks."

"What a stupid boy," said Grandma Maude when she heard. "I hope you wouldn't be that silly, Tim."

Tim shook his head, but he wasn't really listening. Sooner or later, his 'chute would be seen, and recognized. Sarah had almost seen it, just yesterday. He decided to put the scarf back secretly and try to get a flare 'chute like Binky's. But first, he would have one more go.

It was close to tea-time. No one else was at the mound. Tim wound the strings tightly. With a mighty heave, he cast the ball high into the air. The polkadot scarf stood out against the sky as it floated gently down, drifting, lifting occasionally in the breeze. Tim retrieved it and then, he couldn't resist. He scrambled back up onto the mound for one more throw. This time would definitely be his last.

"Tim! Tim!" It was Mum. "Tea-time."

The ball left his hand before he could stop it. It was his best throw. The 'chute soared higher than ever before. At the same time, the breeze freshened. The 'chute opened, lifting, floating away from the back field, to the top of the road. Down it came, down ...

Grandma stood in the garden. She was pointing. "Oh, my!" she cried. "Oh, no! It can't be — Enid! My scarf!"

As Grandma pointed, the wind dropped as suddenly as it had arisen. The polkadot parachute floated gracefully but purposefully into the telephone wires. The weight on the end flipped twice around a wire, and the silk folded down lazily to join it.

Later, as Tim sat on his bed with a plate of bread and a glass of water, he could see the whole thing in his mind once more. It had been a good parachute.

Chapter 10

The Crystal Set

"Take these scraps round to Mrs. Pearson, Tim."

"Okay, Mum."

"Please don't use that slang word, Tim. You know I don't like it."

Tim sighed. He almost said okay in reply, but stopped just in time. He'd heard Mum and other grown-ups complaining about words creeping into the language since the Canadians and Americans had arrived. Tim had to admit he didn't understand some things they said. But what was wrong with that? He shrugged. Grown-ups were funny.

"Hurry up, Tim. Stop day-dreaming. Mrs. Pearson will be making the mash."

Tim pulled on his left boot and tied the lace. "Almost ready, Mum." He pulled on the right boot. "Just got to tie this one and put on my coat."

"Oh, dear. I'll fetch it. Do try to remember to fetch your coat before putting on your boots,

Tim. It's hard work scrubbing this floor."

"Sorry, Mum." Tim really was sorry. He knew Mum was tired.

When Grandma Maude had left, she'd told him to help as much as possible while Mum was pregnant. He wondered what the baby would be. Maybe he'd have a brother soon. He picked up the bowl of vegetable peel and trimmings from the spring greens. Mum's stew last night had been delicious, seasoned with herbs Grandma Maude had left. And Grandma had planted herbs in the back garden that she'd dug from her own garden in Eastbourne. She'd brought seed potatoes too. "Potato Pete will carry us through," she'd said, and, "Doctor Carrot, the children's best friend." Dig for Victory was Grandma's motto. Grandma had sayings for every occasion. Mum said that since the war began, Grandma's sayings had grown and grown, like her garden.

"Off you go then, Tim. And don't be too long," said Mum. "Bill should be here soon."

Tim shook himself. He really was day-dreaming a lot these days. Bill was coming to see them, after visiting Grandma Rose and Grandpa George at Corvuston. Tim wondered if Bill would have the things for the crystal set. "I'm going, Mum."

He shut the back door and strolled down the path. The morning breeze was blowing, and he breathed in deeply. He could smell the aroma of the chicken mash, even though the Pearsons lived two houses down. Perhaps Mr. Pearson would let him feed the chickens this morning. Sometimes he did.

The smell in the Pearsons' kitchen was wonderful. No wonder the chickens laid such good eggs. Mr. Pearson had four White Sussex hens and two cockerels. He'd told Tim that when he got them as chicks he'd thought there were five females and one male. But as they grew, he'd found he had two strutting cocks, with bright red, floppy combs, that gobbled up as much mash between them as the four hens.

"Hello, Tim. Do you want to feed them this morning?"

Tim nodded excitedly. "Yes, please, Mrs. Pearson."

"Well, mind you don't burn yourself. This pot's very hot." Mrs. Pearson smiled. "I'll keep your mum's scraps for tomorrow. Off you go, then."

Steam rose from the open saucepan. The thick, stodgy brown mash smelled delicious. There were all kinds of vegetable scraps in it. There were old eggshells too, and, of course, bran. No wonder the chickens messed all over the place. Tim had tried some mash one day, when he was particularly hungry, and had discovered the fast-acting effect of bran on the bowels. No matter how good the food smelled, he wasn't going to get caught again.

The chickens were gathered at the corner of their pen, clucking excitedly, jostling for position at the galvanized wire mesh. Tim put the saucepan on the ground and took out the wooden spoon. He scooped out a large chunk of mash and took aim. Flick! The steaming ball of food soared up over the wire. The birds whirled round, feet scurrying, wings flapping. Before they reached the food, Tim flicked another ball, steam trailing behind it as it sped over the wire. Five birds wheeled together, heading for this new morsel. One chicken was tucking into the first offering.

Tim continued bombing the chicken-run until the saucepan was clean. It was amazing — none of the chickens ever got hit. That was part of the fun. You could aim three or four balls in quick succession and they'd land all over the place, but the birds always managed to dodge the missiles.

"Tim!" It was Mr. Pearson. "I think that Canadian flying officer is coming up the road."

Tim whirled round.

"Don't forget the saucepan!"

Tim turned and grabbed the long metal handle. The spoon fell and he bent to pick it up. Then he raced down the garden, jumped down the three steps and skidded to a halt at the side door. Mr. Pearson was standing there grinning, his shiny bald head white in the morning sun.

He laughed. "You're in a mighty big hurry."

Tim nodded. "I've got to go, Mr. Pearson. 'Bye."

"Wait up, Tim." Mrs. Pearson came bustling to the door. "Here's your mum's bowl."

"Thank you." Tim took the bowl and charged down the path to the gate. "Bill!" he shouted. "Bill!"

Bill was passing Chalky's house, his kit-bag over his shoulder. He waved with his free hand. "Hi there, Tim."

Soon, all were seated round the shelter. "I got this at the PX," said Bill, "the U.S. canteen. You wouldn't believe the stuff they have. You wouldn't know there's a war on." He pulled a huge tin from his kit-bag, placing it, with a resounding clang, in the middle of the table-shelter.

Mum was pouring tea. "What is it, Bill?"

"Peanut butter."

"What's that?" asked Sarah

Bill smiled. "You tell her, Tim."

Tim shrugged. "I don't know what it is either."

"Don't know what it is?" Bill looked surprised.

"They've never had it, Bill." Mum smiled. "To tell you the truth, I haven't either."

"Hm." Bill took a spoon. Tim held his breath as the lid was pried off. It came free with a metallic pop. But there seemed to be another lid, a shiny, silver seal. Bill ran the lip of the spoon round the edge and lifted off the thin metal cover. "There!" he said triumphantly.

Tim looked at the khaki-coloured substance within. It didn't look like butter and it didn't look very appetizing. Bill dipped the spoon into the tin.

"So, who's first?" He looked disappointed when

no one spoke. They were all staring at the brown glob. "Tim?"

Gingerly, Tim took the spoon and licked it. It wasn't bad. But it didn't taste like butter. He bit off a small mouthful and sucked it. It clung to the roof of his mouth, but it tasted good. He nodded, unable to speak.

"Good?" asked Bill

Tim nodded again. This stuff was difficult to eat. And it made talking hard. He swallowed. "I like it."

"We should have some bread," said Bill, "and some jelly. Sorry, you call it jam."

"Bread, I've got," said Mum, "but jam ..."

"No problem." Bill reached into his kit-bag. He plonked another huge tin on the Morrison. "Strawberry." He opened it. "Sarah?" He held out the spoon. Tim watched, his brown eyes wide and unblinking. This was incredible!

"And that's it," said Bill as they finished tea. He pointed to the array of items on the Morrison. "I had to put the old kite down at a U.S. base last week. If we have to do a pancake — a crash landing, that is —"

"Did you almost crash?" Tim shouted.

Bill nodded. "We were coned, right over the target."

"Coned, Bill?" said Mum. "What's that?"

"It's when the searchlights lock onto you, a bunch of them all together. It's something I dread. We were into our bombing run when they got us. The light was so intense I couldn't see anything, the controls, the instrument panel. I felt totally naked up there."

Tim noticed that Bill's left hand was shaking.

"There were about fifty lights on us, and I knew we were a very shiny target." He shook his head. "I've seen enough bombers coned to know it's no use twisting and turning, hoping to break out of the lights. And I knew that sooner or later, the flak would start up the beams."

"What did you do, Bill?"

"Shoved the nose down hard. Jammed the throttles forward. Only thing to do. I had to outrun those lights."

Sarah was wide-eyed. "What happened, Bill?"

Bill took a deep breath and closed his eyes. He sat back in the chair. "We were in a dive, hurtling down ... an incredible speed. I was worried I might fly us into the ground, so I eased back on the stick." Bill opened his eyes. "Bang! We were hit. The old kite shivered and I lost power. Then again — bang! The window in the cockpit was blown out by a burst of flak. Wonder I wasn't hit. Then, miraculously, we were out of the lights."

Mum and Tim and Sarah sighed.

"But two engines were out," said Bill. "We were crippled and it was a long way home. We were down so low, we were sitting ducks. We had to climb. I took her up. We had to put on our masks, of course."

Tim wanted to ask Bill what the masks were like. Were they like a gas mask? But Bill was continuing.

"It was freezing. Several times I thought my hands were locked onto the controls." Bill had a faraway look. He shrugged and sat quietly, looking out of the window.

Mum was shaking her head. There were tears in her eyes. She took out her handkerchief and blew her nose noisily. "More tea, anyone?"

"Yes, please, Mum." Tim pushed his cup forward. "Then what, Bill?" he asked eagerly.

Bill grinned. "We made it, of course." He chuckled. "So I reckoned we deserved a treat. I found an American field. Always try to find a U.S. base if you have to pancake — the food's great and they allow us to use their PX. So we stocked up on food." Bill smiled. "This is only half of it."

"I don't know how you managed to carry it all," said Mum. Her eyes were red and shiny.

Bill laughed. "Well, I didn't walk out here from Tunbridge Wells this time, that's for sure."

Tim looked at the food — peanut butter, jam, biscuits (Bill called them cookies), tins of corned beef and Spam, two tins of salmon, sugar — and twelve thick bars of chocolate. Tim's mouth watered. Then he looked at the kit-bag. There couldn't be room for anything else.

"Before I forget," said Bill. "Guess what?" He looked round.

"Not more food, surely, Bill?"

Bill smiled. "No, but Sparks did it. He got us a pigeon. We call it Wing Commander Sparklet."

Sarah clapped her hands, then hugged herself. Tim felt like doing the same, but that was babyish. It was good that the bomber crew had a new pigeon, and he liked the name, Wing Commander Sparklet. Then he saw Bill's left hand resting on his knee, shaking. Bill glanced at Tim and looked down. He shook his head and gripped his left hand with the right. He looked away.

"Sparks reckons the pigeon saved us the other night, when we pancaked." Bill shrugged.

"Did he walk round the plane, Bill?" asked Sarah.

Bill nodded. "But only twice. I told him we had to get off in a hurry. But next time he can go three times round, four if he wants to. That's for sure." Bill took a deep breath. "There's another thing." He paused.

"Go on, Bill. What is it?"

"Well, remember I told you about that L.A.C.?"

"You mean Sciver?" said Tim.

Bill nodded. "I'm surprised you remembered that."

"Well, it was after that nasty little fat man chased me round the cemetery," said Tim. "And you said Sciver was a little fat man too. So I remembered."

"You haven't seen that man again, have you, Tim?"

"No, Mum. Just that time."

Bill nodded. "Good thing. Anyway, they caught Sciver. I knew there was something nasty about him."

"What was he doing?" asked Mum.

"Stealing," said Bill. "Stealing of the worst kind. Remember I told you he looked you up and down like an undertaker?"

Tim nodded. "Like before you're buried." He shivered. Thinking about being buried reminded him of the bomb, the Anderson shelter and the gas mask. He had to ask Bill about the mask.

"That's right," said Bill. He pursed his lips, his moustache seeming even more bristly. "He was caught stealing the personal effects of aircrew who were shot down."

"Oh, no!" said Mum.

Bill nodded, his face grim. "Worse still, though, he escaped from custody. Nasty piece of work."

"Well, I hope they catch him and lock him up for good." Mum had little red patches in the middle of her cheeks. She always did when she was really angry. "That really is the lowest of the low. Despicable."

Bill nodded and pushed back his chair. "Now, Tim and I have a project to get on with, and I have to be going soon." He laughed. "So, can we leave the table, Enid?"

Mum smiled. "You may," she said.

"Okay, we wind the wire round and round the tube."

"Like this, Bill?" Tim held the cardboard tube in his left hand, the thin, insulated wire in his right.

"Right, Tim. Keep it nice and tight, but don't cross it over itself. I'll clamp the crystal in this tube."

Tim stopped winding and watched as Bill placed the shiny, black Galena rock into the copper tube. The tube was like a wedding ring, but dull red, the crystal gleaming in places like a diamond. Bill tightened the rock in place with a small screw.

"Sparks made all the pieces for me, so it would be easy to put together."

"I've finished the coil, Bill."

"Good." Bill nodded. A short while later he attached the cat's whisker, twisted the wires from the headset, and soldered them in place. "There."

Mum hadn't been too pleased about the crystal set. It couldn't be kept a secret. The aerial stretched from Tim's bedroom window to the old Bramley apple tree at the bottom of the garden. Bill said the longer the aerial, the stronger the radio signals.

"I'm only letting you have it because Bill would be so disappointed otherwise."

Tim had nodded, saying nothing. But now he could listen to the news each day, and on Sunday he'd listened to "Music While You Work" and "Children's Hour." Then, one day, when he'd moved the cat's whisker on the crystal and the small metal bead on the tuning coil to find a clearer signal, he'd picked up a foreign station. The words were a jumble and the signal whistled and popped and faded, but Bill had been right — with the old military earphones, he did feel like a pilot in a Lancaster bomber, or a prisoner of war. Bill had told him that prisoners built sets to pick up news from England. Maybe Dad had one. Tim sighed.

"And I don't want you listening to it after eight o'clock," Mum had said. "Is that clear, Tim?"

Inwardly, Tim groaned. ITMA came on at eight. "Yes, Mum," he'd said, crossing his fingers behind his back. Maybe he might listen, just once a week, on Thursdays. Surely that couldn't hurt?

A week later, huddled down in his bed, the covers pulled over his head, he picked up ITMA, broadcast from the army theatre, The Garrison, at Woolwich. If Dad had been home, he'd have been there, Tim was sure.

Chapter 11

The Three-legged Man

Spring was in the air. Tim wandered up to the back field. No one was there. Lizards, basking in the sun on a pile of old bricks, scurried into hiding as he approached. Tim had thought of keeping a lizard as a pet, but Mum wouldn't hear of it. Tim missed Bits, even though it was years since that dreadful night. Dad had been heartbroken, but he wouldn't buy another dog. "Wait until the war is over," he'd said. "It won't be long." Tim sighed. It didn't look as if the war would ever end.

The potato mound was gone, the sods of grass relaid to cover the bared ground. It would be a few months before the farmer built a new one. Tim nodded. He must remember to ask Bill about flare parachutes. In all the excitement of the last visit, he'd forgotten again.

"Hello, Tim." Angela, one of the bigger girls,

was coming up the hillside that ran behind the houses. It stretched up from Granger's Woods, along the back field, into the distance.

"Hello, Angela. Have you seen Binky?"

Angela shook her head. "He might be in the hollow. I saw some boys down there." She shrugged. "They're stupid. I wouldn't go there."

"Thanks, Angela." Tim set off at a jog. Binky had told him that there was a funny old man living in a ramshackle house by the hollow. No one went near him, Tim wasn't sure why. What was Binky doing there? Tim rounded the blackthorn hedge that grew behind the houses. In the distance he saw the boys, halfway down the hill.

They weren't actually in the hollow. Tim slowed down, scuffing his boots in the grass. It was getting quite long now. There were tender green shoots and new leaves on the hawthorn, intermingled with the blackthorn. He picked some to nibble. Bread and cheese — that's what Dad called them. Tim didn't think the leaves tasted anything like bread and cheese.

There was the chink, chink, chink of a blackbird, the danger call. Tim always thought of it as the bird's air-raid warning. At first he took little notice. Then the first bird was joined by others, fluttering round a particular spot. Tim stopped. He stood very still, waiting. A pointed little face with beady eyes peered out from the lower branches of the hedge. It didn't notice Tim for all the chatter of the birds. Tim looked for the tail. It was long with a black tip. What had Dad said? "A weasel has a short, brown tail."

So this was a stoat. It caught his scent and darted back into hiding. Tim hissed. Dad said if you did that, the stoat might come back to investigate. This one didn't.

Tim continued on. He whistled. Dad had taught him to whistle, a soft, lilting sound. He didn't blow out like most people, but sucked in gently. A little moisture on the middle of his tongue made a slight warbling noise, just like a bird. He remembered once, when he was very small, he'd tried to whistle like the milkman, blowing out. The milkman, his bottles clinking and jangling in their wooden crate, always whistled as he came striding up the path. That day, Tim was sucking a liquorice allsort. He blew hard. All that came out was the liquorice. It landed in the dirt, and even when he'd wiped it off, it didn't taste very good.

Tim sighed. It was a glorious day. If only Dad was here. A lone Spitfire droned high overhead, tracing a filmy, milky-white trail of condensation across the sky. Tim watched until his eyes grew tired in the sunlight.

He was closer to the boys now. He saw Chalky White and hoped Binky was there. A boy pointed at him and tugged at Chalky's sleeve. Chalky laughed. Then Tim heard someone crying. It must be one of the younger boys. Binky said Chalky was always making the smaller boys do things they didn't want to do.

Tim stopped. He looked round hurriedly. There was no sign of Binky, and none of the boys here were Binky's friends. There was definitely something wrong. That crying ... It was Sarah! Chalky White strode up the slope, his head cocked on one side. "Where's Binky, then?" His lower lip was thrust out aggressively. "Where's your big friend?"

"Tim!" shouted Sarah. "They're taking me to the three-legged man!" She started to cry again.

"You leave my sister alone!" said Tim.

Chalky came closer, advancing up the slope. He laughed. It was a nasty sound, short and sharp, matching the mean look in his eyes. "Say 'sir' when you speak to me."

Tim stared at him. He had to do something. He had to look after Sarah. But he was worried. There was no help in sight. "Just you leave my sister alone!"

Chalky's eyes gleamed and he leered. "You call me sir!" he shouted, his head thrust forward, his forefinger jabbing Tim in the chest. "You — call — me — sir!" With each word he gave a short, hard poke with his finger.

Tim stood his ground. Chalky's jabs hurt him, but he wasn't going to show it. Some of the boys moved forward.

"Say it!" Chalky leaned closer. "Come on, say it!"

Tim swallowed hard. Maybe he could rush Chalky like he had before. But Chalky was too close. Tim backed up the slope a few steps. That was better. Chalky was laughing, his head thrown back. It had to be now! Tim charged down the slope and thrust his elbow into Chalky's side. He kept on running toward the crowd ahead, as Chalky collapsed on the ground, doubled up and gasping for breath. Tim grabbed Sarah's arm and dragged her, stumbling, behind him.

They were almost in the hollow when the cry went up. Chalky had recovered sufficiently to scramble to his feet. Staggering and clutching at his side, he was leading the small gang down the slopes. Some were making war whoops.

"Get them!" shouted Chalky, breathlessly.

Tim looked desperately from side to side. There was no way out of the hollow. Ahead was a tangled hedge of hawthorn, brambles and rose brier; behind, his pursuers. Tim was desperate. Then he saw a narrow gap in the hedge.

"Not there!" cried Sarah. "Not in there! That's where the three-legged man lives."

For a moment, Tim hesitated. Then he made his decision. He pulled Sarah toward the opening. She burst into tears, tugging at his arm, dragging her feet.

"We have to, Sarah!" Tim pushed through the gap. Brambles tore at his coat, scratching his legs. "Come on!"

The running behind them stopped and there was whispering. Then the running started again, but this time going away. Tim peered through the hedge. Chalky's gang was running up the slopes, Chalky hobbling along behind, holding his side. Tim shrugged. He turned back. Through some currant bushes he could see a figure, unmoving.

Bees buzzed round the head. It must be a scarecrow. Beneath a wide-brimmed hat was a blank, cloth face. Hanging from square shoulders was a shapeless black cloak. And beneath the coat were legs in black ...

Tim's heart missed a beat. There were three legs! As Tim watched in horror, this monstrous apparition turned, the outside leg rising off the ground, thick grey smoke hissing, billowing from the bootless end. It was the three-legged man! More smoke belched from the black, bootless tube. The bees flew off.

Sarah screamed, and Tim felt his blood turn to ice.

"There, there, lass," said a muffled but kindly voice. "No need to cry. I'll not hurt ye."

Sarah clung to Tim's arm, sobbing.

The monster took off his hat. The cloth came away with it, a thick veil of fine net, revealing a gentle face beneath a mass of curly grey hair.

The lower half of the face was hidden by a moustache and beard. Deep blue eyes twinkled.

"Now, what's all this? And who are ye?"

Sarah stopped sobbing and stared at this strange apparition. "Why have you got that funny leg?" she said.

"Leg?" The man in black looked down. "Ah ha! You mean this." He held up the long tube that Tim now saw was hooked to a thick leather belt. There was a hiss, and smoke poured out of the end.

Sarah screamed and jumped back, hiding behind Tim, clinging now to his coat.

"Sorry," said the man. "I didn't mean to frighten ye. I'll turn it off. My bees are quietened down now." He unhooked the thick tube and placed it beside a box on the ground. Tim could now see a thinner tube leading from the box to the large tube he'd mistaken for a third trouser leg. Now he could see that the end was actually a large funnel. There was another hiss and more smoke.

"There, that should be fine. Now, ye were about to tell me why ye're here."

"They said you were a three-legged man," said Tim.

The man's bushy eyebrows shot up, his eyes opened wide. "Ho! Ho! Ho!" The face behind the beard was going red. "Hee, hee, hee." The man started to wheeze and cough.

"Are you all right?" asked Tim.

The man stopped coughing and wiped his eyes with a rag. He started to laugh again. Tim liked it. It was a deep, friendly sound. "The three-legged man, ye say? Hee, hee."

"My sister was jolly scared," said Tim. He wasn't going to admit that he'd been frightened too.

The man nodded and wiped his eyes again. "I can tell that. But, as ye can well see, I'm not a monster, I'm a beekeeper. See." He pointed to some white boxes standing on short wooden legs. "That's where my bees live."

Tim was fast losing all fear. "You mean you keep them as pets?"

"Well, not pets exactly. But come with me." The man held out a grubby, gnarled hand. "Come on. Ye too, lassy. Ye 'ave no reason to be frightened of me."

Sarah poked her head out from behind Tim. She looked at the beekeeper and then at Tim. He nodded.

"Come along, then." The man led them through a well-tended garden to a ramshackle old cottage. "Now, let's see what we can find. How about some tea, and bread and butter sandwiches?"

"Do you have any treacle, sir?" asked Tim.

"Not treacle, laddy. But I think I might be able to find something."

The cottage was cool and not as tumbledown inside as out. The wooden floor of the kitchen was highly polished and the oak table scrubbed almost white. Sparkling dishes were stacked on shelves in an old shiny cupboard. The beekeeper put the kettle on a white enamelled stove and lit a gas burner. Blue flame spread out gently beneath the copper surface, and soon the kettle began to sing.

"Now, young man, what's thy name?"

"Tim. Timothy Athelstan, sir. And this is my sister, Sarah."

"Pleased to meet thee." The man held out his hand. "I'm Mr. Runciman. Now, who told ye this tale of a three-legged man?"

"It was Chalky," said Sarah. "He told me."

"And who might this Chalky be?" asked Mr. Runciman. "I don't get out much to meet people these days."

Tim explained how Chalky was a bully and how he'd first met him.

"I see." Mr. Runciman nodded, slowly. "And what were ye doing with them, young lassy?"

Tim listened as Sarah explained. Chalky had tricked Sarah by saying that Tim was down the slopes. When Sarah went to find him, Chalky and the others followed. "He said that because you'd hit him, he was going to punish me, throw me to the three-legged man."

Tim was angry. Chalky was a rotten bully.

"Disgusting!" said the beekeeper. "A big boy like that taking revenge on a little girl." He snorted. "I can't believe it."

"But it's true," said Sarah.

Mr. Runciman nodded. "I didn't mean I thought ye were lying, Sarah. Ye are lucky to have a plucky young brother to take care of ye."

Tim felt a warm feeling inside. He hadn't thought of it like that, but it was true. He had taken care of Sarah. Dad would be pleased if he knew.

The kettle whistled shrilly. "Ah. A cup of tea will do us good." Mr. Runciman shook his head. "I still can't believe it." He busied himself at the counter. "Now, I don't have treacle, but I do have honey." He placed a large earthenware pot on the table, then a smaller pot and a round loaf. "Don't be shy. Cut a thick slice. And that's real butter, not that margarine mixture. Right. Now some honey." Tim watched in awe as a large wooden spoon, dripping with thick amber liquid, was held over the buttered bread. "Now, eat up, the pair of ye."

Chapter 12

Run, Rabbit, Run!

"And then Tim saved me, Mummy."

Mrs. Athelstan nodded. "Well, I'm glad it's over and all sorted out. I'd no idea where you were. And then Mrs. White was at my door, accusing Tim of attacking her boy."

"But I didn't attack him, Mum, not really."

"I know that now, Tim, but at the time I didn't know where you were, and the boy is injured."

Tim nodded. Chalky had two broken ribs, and the doctor had bound him up with wide bands of sticking plaster. It would be awful when they had to pull them off. But Chalky wouldn't be bullying anyone for a long time.

"Tim didn't mean to break his chest, Mummy."

"His ribs, dear. I know." Mum smiled and ran her fingers through Sarah's long fair hair. "When Mrs. White saw him bent over, taking shallow breaths and wheezing, she thought Brian might have asthma like his father."

"Is that his name, Mum?"

"You mean Brian? Didn't you know that?"

Tim shook his head. "Everyone calls him Chalky."

"Well, his name is Brian, Tim. And I gather he's a very unhappy lad. But that doesn't excuse his bullying, at least not in my book. I told his mother that."

"What did she say, Mum?"

"She agreed. She's really quite a nice lady. Somehow I got the feeling that things are difficult for everyone in that house." Mum shook her head slowly.

"Is it because Chalky's dad's ill?"

"That's part of it, Tim. He can't join up because of his asthma."

"My friend John's got asthma and he's all right," said Tim.

Mum nodded. "It affects people differently. Mrs. White told me that Mr. White's been in hospital several times. He almost died when he was a boy." She sighed. "But they don't have to worry about him fighting overseas. They don't have to worry if he's missing or ..." Mum's voice was a whisper. She looked out of the window and was silent.

Tim thought about this. He wasn't sure if he'd rather have a dad who was sick, or one able to fight in the war. He knew, somehow, that Dad wouldn't want to be sick. But he did wish Dad was here.

Mum was speaking again. "Mr. White did try to enlist several times. He even tried the Home Guard and the Air Raid Patrol, but they couldn't risk having him either."

"Why not, Mum?"

"In case he had an asthma attack, Tim. You see, he can't go near smoke. And he can't wear a gas mask."

Tim's throat went tight, his mouth dry. He could feel the clammy, sweaty touch of the thick black rubber, breathe the cloying smell of the hated mask.

Mum was continuing. "Mrs. Pearson told me that, as a boy, he couldn't join in with the others, couldn't go out on Guy Fawkes Night."

That was terrible. There hadn't been a real Guy Fawkes Night since the war began. Tim remembered the last time, with the fireworks and the bonfire, and the brightly painted papier mâché mask with the big black moustache. He wondered if he'd ever be able to wear a Guy Fawkes mask again. He hated to think of anything over his face. He must change the subject.

"Do you like Mr. Runciman, Mum?"

Mum smiled. "He does seem a nice old man. But they say he's a bit of a recluse."

"What's a recluse?" asked Tim.

"Someone who usually lives alone and doesn't

like other people bothering them."

"Oh. I expect that's why he blows smoke at anyone who goes near his place," said Tim.

Mum smiled again. "As I understand it, that story started one summer, many years ago, when he had a large swarm of bees. Some boys were raiding his garden for strawberries, or something like that. Mrs. Pearson told me about it. Anyway, the boys would have been stung by hundreds of bees if Mr. Runciman hadn't blown smoke at them."

"You mean he's got hundreds of bees in those boxes, Mummy?"

"That's right, Sarah. Each box is like a bee town. Anyway, the boys were busy gathering berries when the bees swarmed and Mr. Runciman came up with his smoke box. They didn't see him at first, and he didn't see them. The bees frightened them. Then they saw Mr. Runciman with all his protective clothing, and the smoke, of course. They ran off screaming. From then on, the story of the three-legged man spread. Even though it happened years ago, Mrs. Pearson said none of the youngsters round here will go near his house."

"That's silly," said Sarah. "He's nice."

"Well, with that tube," said Tim, "and all his black clothes and the mask ... It was scary, Mum. And when I saw him, I really did think he had three legs, at first."

Sarah nodded. "So did I. I was scared then."

Mrs. Athelstan nodded. "I know, dear."

Tim laughed. "I like him. He says we can go round any time we want to, and he'll give us more honey and —"

"That doesn't mean you have to finish it all in one go, Tim. That's too much. It will drip all over the tablecloth. I don't have enough soap flakes to do any more washing, and I certainly don't have enough bread." Mum pushed her chair back. "Now, let's clear this up."

Tim took his plate and cup to the large wooden sink. He put the rubber plug in the drain hole and turned on the hot tap, holding a small wire cage with scraps of soap inside it under the running water. Bubbles began to form on the surface.

There was knock at the front door.

"That's unusual," said Mum. "No one calls at the front door here."

"I'll get it." Tim turned off the tap and put the soap cage on the grooved wooden draining board. He walked down the hall, running his fingers along the cream-painted bannister rails. There was a second knock as he reached for the handle. And there stood Bill.

"Bill!" Tim shouted. "Mum, it's Bill!"

"So I hear. And I should think the whole neighbourhood will know, too." Mum laughed.

And the story of the three-legged man was retold over more tea.

"By the way, Bill, have they caught that horrible little man?" Mum asked as they washed up.

"The L.A.C. — Sciver, you mean?" Bill shook his head. He picked up a saucer and gave it an extra hard rub with the wiping-up cloth. "No, he seems to have disappeared. I hope they get him soon. It was quite a shock for the guys to think he'd stolen personal things belonging to friends, and could have stolen theirs if they'd ditched or had a prang. Some of the things were presents from wives, girlfriends ... You know." Bill looked grim, his mouth a hard, straight line beneath his fair moustache. "It would be a real boost to morale to have that little swine behind bars." He picked up the last cup, wiping it so hard Tim thought the handle would come off. "Now, you said you wanted some wood, Enid."

Mum nodded. "That's right, Bill. This old stove eats it, so does the copper. I'm still boiling clothes we rescued after the bombing, trying to get them clean."

"There's still plenty of wood down the hill, Mum." Tim looked out of the window. "If we hurry we could get some before it gets dark."

"Can I go?" asked Sarah.

"Well, I —"

"Sure she can, Enid." Bill picked up Sarah and placed her on his shoulders. She giggled and held onto his hair. "Hey, watch that, young lady, you'll have me bald before my time." Bill laughed. "Why don't you come too, Enid? The more the merrier."

Tim was annoyed. He'd wanted Bill to himself, to talk about the crystal set and ask about the masks the crew wore in the bomber. And he must remember flare parachutes.

"You know, I think I will," Mum was saying. "It will do me good to get out for a walk, without thinking about food and coupons and ..."

It was the first time Tim had seen Mum really happy in weeks.

"Well, let's hit the road," said Bill. "Get that chopper, Tim. And this time we'll do things sensibly. We'll bring it back in lengths, then I'll cut it to size. Do you have any rope, Enid?"

"There's some in the shed," said Tim. "I've seen it. I'll get my coat."

"Okay," said Bill. "And tomorrow, before I leave, I'll get two, maybe three more loads. You'll have to cut them to size, Tim."

"That will really help, Bill." Mum smiled.

By the time Bill was satisfied with the pile of wood, the evening sun was beginning to sink behind the slopes. In the distance, the back field took on a delicate shade of pink. Most of the people cutting wood had left, some with wheelbarrows, some with bicycles, the lengths of wood tied to the crossbars. A few remained. Tim eyed the cut wood with concern. How could they carry it all?

"We'll make two bundles," said Bill. "One for you, Tim, and one for me. We'll drag them, not carry them."

Tim nodded. That made sense. Pulling them up the hill would be much easier.

Mum smiled. "I can manage a small load."

Bill shook his head. "No way, Enid. Not in your condition. Aunt Rose would never feed me again if she heard I'd let you do anything."

Mum nodded. "She's right, I suppose."

"What about me?" asked Sarah.

"Ah. I was coming to that." Bill picked up the chopper. "You have the most important job, carrying the woodsman's trusty axe. But be careful, it's sharp."

Bill was holding out the chopper when a rabbit darted from beneath a bundle of wood. It ran for the trees. Bill spun round and threw the chopper, straight as a die. The rabbit fell prone on the ground. Tim could hardly believe his eyes. Then he heard people cheering.

One older man shouted, "Nice shot, Canada! That Adolf Hitler had better watch out."

Everyone was laughing, except Sarah. She was crying. "I don't want to carry that chopper."

Bill nodded slowly. "I understand, Sarah, believe me." He sighed.

"Then why did you do that?" Sarah looked up out of glistening, dark brown eyes. "Why did you kill it?"

Tim felt sorry for the rabbit, but he was proud of Bill. He could hardly wait to tell Binky. Why couldn't Sarah understand?

"Bill was thinking of us, dear," said Mum. "That rabbit will make a delicious stew."

"I don't want any," said Sarah. "I won't eat it."

Mum looked at Bill. "I'll take her home. Can you two manage the wood by yourselves?"

Bill nodded slowly. "Sorry about that, Enid."

Mum shook her head. "Don't be, Bill. And please bring the rabbit. I'll not let good food go to waste. It's difficult enough these days. Tomorrow she'll be over it ... and hungry."

"Right." Bill smiled weakly. "See you guys a little later." He turned. "Let's examine our catch, Tim."

Chapter 13

The Penny Spitfire

"Sarah will be all right the next time you're here, Bill."

"I sure hope so, Tim."

Tim was walking Bill to the bus stop. It was a lovely evening, but clouds massed in the distance, heading toward Medbury.

They neared the top of the hill. The horse chestnut by the gate to Limekiln Farm was a magnificent sight, bursting with fresh leaves and white blossoms that had flowered during the past week.

"Lovely tree," said Bill.

"It's one of the biggest I've ever seen," said Tim. "It's even bigger than the old tree Dad and I used to go to on Hampstead Heath." He nodded. "There should be lots of conkers. I had a four-hundred-and-sixtier last year."

"Four-hundred-what?" said Bill. "I don't get it."

"You know," said Tim. "Iddy, Iddy Onker, my first conker. You must have played conkers when you were a boy."

Bill shook his head. "Conkers? No. Can't say I remember."

Tim was amazed. Everybody knew what conkers were. "Don't you have conker trees in Canada?" he asked.

"Horse chestnuts, you mean?"

Tim shrugged. "That's their proper name, but we just call them conkers."

"Hm." Bill nodded. "There are horse chestnuts in the park at St. Catharines. My cousin, Joan, used to make necklaces with them, before they moved to White Rock."

"How far away is White Rock?" said Tim.

"From here, you mean? Over seven thousand miles," said Bill.

Tim had trouble understanding how far that was. "How much farther is it than flying to Germany?"

Bill was silent for a moment. He pursed his lips and breathed in deeply. His left hand was shaking. He thrust it into his coat pocket. "It depends," he said. "From our base to Bremen is about three hundred and fifty miles. To Berlin, it's six hundred. Just to reach Canada you'd have to fly five times as far as to Berlin."

"Phew! That's a long way."

"Sure is," said Bill. He looked up at the darkening sky and shivered. "Flying to Berlin is far enough. Too far sometimes. I'll be glad when this tour is over."

"When will that be?" asked Tim.

"About a month, I guess. Yep." Bill pursed his lips again. "Another month." He shook himself as if trying to get warm. "Anyway, you were telling me about playing conkers."

Tim nodded. "Well, you get a conker — that's the brown nut. You drill a hole through, with a skewer, and —"

Bill interrupted. "A skewer?"

Tim nodded. "A meat skewer. You know, the twisty kind. You have to be careful not to get it in your hand."

Bill looked confused.

"And you thread a thick piece of string through the hole and tie a big knot in the end. If you have a cheesy, the knot has to be really big. And sometimes you soak it in vinegar and put it in the oven, and —"

"Hold it right there, Tim. I thought you said this was a game. What's this about meat skewers, and butchers, and cheese, and vinegar, and the oven?"

Tim looked up at Bill. "The oven and vinegar make it hard, so it will break the other person's conker more easily." Tim shrugged. He'd thought everyone knew that.

"I still don't get it," said Bill.

Tim shook his head. It wasn't easy explaining without conkers. He thought for a few moments. "Perhaps I'd better show you when the conkers are ripe. Then we can have a game, and I'll show you about stringsies and things."

Bill chuckled. "I think that's the best idea, Tim. With skewers and cheese and vinegar — you've lost me."

They walked on silently, past the butcher's and the greengrocer's, nearing the village green. As they came to the church, Bill stopped, looking up at the sky, his head cocked to one side. There was a faint hum in the distance. Bill nodded, his lips pressed hard together. Almost to himself he said, "I wonder what the target is tonight?"

Tim listened. The hum drew nearer, turning to a steady drone, then a throbbing roar as the planes passed overhead, hidden by thick, grey cloud.

"Were they Lancasters?" asked Tim.

"Yep. Can't mistake the throb of those four engines," said Bill. "Great kite, but heavy, lumbering old bird. When this tour's over, I'm going to see if I can change from bombers to fighters. There's a Canadian Spitfire squadron — Wolf Squadron — based at Kenley, just south of London. And that reminds me." He reached into the breast pocket of his tunic and pulled out a handkerchief. "I almost forgot." He unwrapped the cloth. In the centre was a small, shiny copper model of a fighter plane. Bill lifted it between forefinger and thumb. "Here, Tim." He held it up. On the underside was a safety-pin, attached by a line of solder. "Let me pin it on for you."

Tim's eyes were wide. "Is it for me?"

Bill nodded. "I got Sparks to make it. He's clever like that." He grinned. "It cost me, though."

Tim looked at the tiny plane. "Did it cost a lot?"

Bill laughed, that deep, rumbling sound Tim liked to hear. He paused, his eyes twinkling. "Cost me a whole penny." He laughed again. "Sparks makes them out of pennies. He calls them his penny Spitfires."

Tim touched the shiny copper plane pinned to his coat, his fingers feeling the smooth red metal. A penny Spitfire. It wasn't easy to see at that angle, but it really did look like a miniature fighter. "Thank you, Bill." He paused. "Can I ask you something?"

"Sure. Fire away."

"You know you said about having to wear a mask, when you'd been coned and the flak hit you?"

Bill nodded. "Yep. Had to put on our oxygen masks, to be able to breathe."

"Is it like a gas mask?"

Again, Bill nodded. "Sort of, Tim. Yes. It's made of rubber. Fits over your nose and mouth."

Tim shuddered. He could smell the rubber, the

tight, choking mask. He swallowed. "Do you like wearing it, Bill? I hate my gas mask. It makes me feel as if I'm going to suffocate."

Bill looked down. "Mm. I see. Now you mention it, it is a bit like that. But you haven't worn a gas mask for ages, surely? I can't remember seeing anyone carrying one."

It was true. They hadn't had a practice at school for the longest time. Tim shook his head. "It's just when I think of masks I get that feeling." He looked up. It wasn't so bad, now that he was talking about it. But he wondered if Bill would think him a baby, not liking the gas mask.

Bill rested his left hand on Tim's shoulder. There was a slight tremor, and Tim knew the hand was shaking.

"I know what you mean, Tim. I didn't like it at first. No one likes to feel ... well, trapped." Bill looked up at the darkening sky. "Sometimes, especially when you're in charge, like I'm in charge of L-for-Lucky Lancaster, you have to do things you don't want to, to help others. You see, Tim, up there the guys rely on me to get them home safely. Do you see what I mean? I might not like the mask, but if I didn't wear it, I'd pass out, crash the old kite."

Tim nodded thoughtfully. But maybe ... He heard the whine of the bus.

"Hey!" Bill removed his hand from Tim's shoulder. "Is that the bus? I daren't miss it." He started to run, shouting over his shoulder. "See you next month, Tim."

Tim started to run too, but Bill was now racing ahead, past the lych-gate, his kit-bag bouncing up and down. He reached the bus stop just in time, turned, waved, and jumped onto the platform.

Tim stopped running, watching as the bus pulled away. "'Bye, Bill!" he shouted. "'Bye, Bill!" He waved, watching the bus disappear into the dusk, into the trees. All was quiet. Mum had said to come straight home, but he stood there for a while, an ache in his throat, feeling the tiny plane pinned to his lapel. A heavy drop of rain fell, splattering on his hand, then another. He turned and ran.

PART 2

TAILS OF FLAME

Chapter 14

Rags and Bones

For three days, the khaki-clad Canadian soldiers had been camped in the back field. They'd arrived on Monday, and set about draping the bren gun carriers, armoured cars, anti-tank guns and field guns with camouflage netting. They were on manoeuvres, and every night Tim could hear the men marching down Granger Park Road to the valley beyond Limekiln Farm. In the early morning, he heard them return, the steady beat of marching feet and the occasional muffled voice waking him from sleep. It felt safe to have them around, and he would climb out of bed, draw back the curtains and duck under the blackout, watching them tramp up the road to the back field once more.

Tim hadn't spoken to any of them yet. They were asleep before he set off for school. Every morning, he waved to the sentries patrolling at the top of the road, and breathed in the cooking smells still hanging on the morning air. Smelling that delicious food made him feel hungry all day. And on Monday, the day after the troops arrived, he couldn't go up to the back field because of the loaf.

Tim hadn't meant to eat the loaf. That Monday, when he got off the bus, he went to the baker's for Mum. Sarah walked ahead with the girls, and Tim strolled leisurely down the road. The smell of the fresh bread whet his appetite, and he started taking small pieces from one end of the loaf, almost without realizing that he was doing so.

Sarah was waiting for him at the end of the road. "Mummy wants the bread, Tim. Give it to me."

Tim reached into his satchel and pulled out the loaf. It had collapsed in the middle, and there was an enormous hole in one end. Sarah's eyes widened.

"I'm not taking it." She shook her head. "Mummy's going to be mad at you." And she ran off up the road.

A short while later, Tim was in his room with only a glass of water for dinner.

Then on Tuesday he had to stay at school and write lines. It was that rotten milk again. It was good in tea, but by itself it was awful. He'd been caught swapping the small, unopened bottle for marbles with one of the First Form boys. Five hundred lines: *I must drink my milk.*

Mum was upset that he was late, and he only just managed to avoid another night without dinner.

But Wednesday was worse. Now Tim knew why Monica, the red-haired girl, had that smell. It wasn't her hair. He was sitting on the bench next to her, as far away as possible, while Sister Mary Paul pointed to a map of Africa.

"This is Nyasaland." She moved the pointer down slightly. "And this is Northern Rhodesia. A lot of children here have very little to eat."

Tim felt a strange, warm sensation on his right thigh. He looked down. He couldn't believe his eyes. Running along the bench, from Monica to himself, was a puddle. He glared at the red-haired girl. She looked away, avoiding his eyes, her face as red as her hair. Tim jumped up, feeling his wet trousers and staring down at the seat. Monica burst into tears.

Sister Mary Paul came striding down the aisle, black robes flowing behind her. She looked in horror at the bench and then reached down and felt Tim's leg. "Oh! Oh! You horrible, nasty little boy! Oh! You should go to the toilet before class starts!"

"But —"

"Be quiet, Athelstan! Go to the kitchen, right now! Ask sister for a bucket and cloth. And clean that up!"

"But —"

"Quiet!" The teacher patted Monica's head. "It's all right, dear." She glared at Tim. "Now, Athelstan! And ask Sister Joseph to put plenty of disinfectant in the water!" Her eyes behind the wire-rimmed glasses bored into Tim, and her nose seemed to quiver. She turned to Monica. "There, there, dear. I'll move you away from this horrid boy." She glared at Tim again. "We'll find another seat."

"But —" Tim couldn't believe what he was hearing.

"No buts, Athelstan! Do as I say! Now!"

Cleaning the bench was awful. Everyone looked at him. And at lunch time it took ages to convince even some of his best friends that he hadn't wet himself — it was stinky old Monica. Then, just as it was time to go home, Sister had told him to write out lines again, five hundred times:

I must go to the toilet before class.

I must go to the toilet before class.

I must ...

"I believe you, Tim," said Mum. "But you can't go up to the back field now, your dinner's ready."

So it wasn't until Thursday that Tim met the troops. As he neared the back field with Binky, the soldiers suddenly started to cheer.

"Hi, Binky," called one of the young men. "We've just heard the news."

"What news?" said Binky.

"The Gustave Line." The soldier smiled. "We've captured Cassino. The Hun's retreating to Rome." He stopped talking, looking down at Tim. "What's the matter, youngster?"

"My dad was there," said Tim, "until February. Then he was sent to Anzio. He's missing."

The soldier nodded. "I see. He's a prisoner."

Tim shook his head. "We don't know. Mum just had a telegram saying he was missing."

"Ah." The young soldier looked round. Nearby, the rest of the soldiers were talking excitedly. "Well, if I had to guess, I'd bet your dad's hiding out somewhere."

"That's what I keep telling him," said Binky.

The soldier nodded. "I bet that's what he's doing. And now we've broken the Hun at Cassino, he may be able to get back to his unit."

Tim looked down at his boots. Perhaps the soldier was right. Maybe they'd hear from Dad soon.

"Yep. That's what I'd try to do," the soldier continued. "As soon as our guys moved up, I'd head back to join the fight." He smiled, and ruffled Tim's unruly fair hair. "Cheer up. We've got to celebrate."

"My uncle's a Canadian." Tim didn't know why he said it. He just knew he had to change the subject. It hurt to think about Dad, in case he wasn't safe.

"So where's your uncle from?" asked the soldier.

"He's not actually my uncle," said Tim. "He's my dad's cousin. He comes from Ontario."

"Ha. That's where we're from. Where in Ontario?"

"I think it's a place called St. Catharines."

"Well, would you believe it? Hey, you guys."

The soldier called to his friends. "This youngster has a cousin from St. Catharines." He turned to Tim. "What's his name?"

"Bill," said Tim. "He's a bomber pilot. He was here two weeks ago." Other men began to gather round.

"A bomber pilot." The soldier nodded. "What's his last name?"

"Brewer," said Tim. "Like in the song about Widdecombe Fair. Bill Brewer."

"Bill Brewer? Well, would you believe it?" Another young soldier pushed forward through the crowd. "Bill and I went to school together, played hockey. Lucky devil, Bill. I couldn't get into the RCAF — my eyes." He smiled. "Next time you see Bill, tell him that Cherry was here."

"Cherry?" said Tim, not sure he'd heard right.

The soldier nodded. "My cheeks. When I play hockey, I get red cheeks." He laughed. "So they call me Cherry."

It was Saturday. The Canadian soldiers were gone. Tim had watched from his window as the vehicles rumbled slowly down the road during the night. He thought he'd seen Cherry wave from an armoured car, but he wasn't sure.

Now the back field was empty, the grass crushed and flattened. Here and there were long, low, narrow mounds of fresh earth, where trenches had been dug and filled.

Tim and Binky and some other children searched the field and the orchard for souvenirs, for anything left by the soldiers. They'd been at it for hours, or so it seemed, and nobody had found much of anything. Most of the children left. Tim sat on the ground, bored. Binky was at the far end of the field, near the orchard. Tim shifted, and his hand came to rest on something small but hard. He looked down and there beneath his fingers was a cap badge. At that moment, Binky came racing back toward him.

"Do you hear him?" shouted Binky.

Tim hurriedly shoved the badge into his pocket. "Hear who?"

"The rag and bone man. That's his bell."

Tim stood up, his hand thrusting the badge as deeply into his pocket as he could. He wanted to be sure that it wouldn't fall out. "What's so important about the rag and bone man?"

Binky shrugged. "Nothing really, I suppose. It's just that he's a funny old geezer. He's got the baldest head you've ever seen. It's balder than old Pearson's. He's only got a few strands of greasy, grey hair in patches at the back. He's got the worst teeth you ever did see, jagged and stained. And he smells. He smells like all the rotten stuff in his cart. Mum saves all our bones for him."

"Bones?" said Tim. "You mean to make glue?"

"No." Binky looked at him in surprise. "They don't use them for glue anymore. They're for cordite."

Tim vaguely remembered Grandma Maude talking about bones and cordite.

"A chop bone, even after it's been boiled for stock, will make enough cordite to fire two shells from a Hurricane's guns," said Binky.

Now Tim remembered. That's what Grandma had said. She was always talking about things like that. She'd say, "A six-inch end of darning wool from every house in Britain will make six hundred battledress uniforms. Twenty-four rusty keys will make a hand grenade. Forty-two will make a steel helmet. And one rusty key from every house would make twelve tanks!"

Tim didn't know why the keys had to be rusty. And every little piece of soap was saved and put into the small, wire container by the kitchen sink. "Waste not, want not," Grandma said. "You can use that for washing up."

"I remember," said Tim. And he followed Binky to the top of the road.

"Rag'n bones! Rag'n bones!" The man was dirty, unshaven, long stubble masking his face. He wore a filthy cap pulled down over his eyes. But his teeth were white, and thick, mousy-brown hair, not grey, grew out from under the cap and curled over his ears. He was outside Bramley Cottage.

"We don't have anything," Mum was saying. "We were bombed out just three months ago."

"Hm. Want anything sharpenin'?"

Mum nodded. "As a matter of fact, I do." She saw Tim. "Fetch the chopper for me, please."

Tim ran up the path to the coal bunker. The chopper was by the pile of wood that he and Bill had split and chopped. He took out the badge and gave it a furtive look. He'd hardly had time to make out the word Lincoln when Mum called, "Tim! Tim! Do hurry up."

"Coming," he shouted back, returning the badge to his pocket. He raced back down the pathway to the gate. "Here it is, Mum."

The man had set up a stone wheel and treadle at the back of the cart. He took the chopper and ran his finger down the edge of the blade.

"That's not the old geezer," whispered Binky. "It's the old man's cart, all right, but that's not him."

The sandstone wheel began to spin as the rag and bone man pressed his foot up and down on the wooden pedal. Sparks flew from the wheel. The steel blade of the chopper screamed as it was run across the stone. It made Tim's teeth ache. He shivered. It was like chalk scraping on a blackboard.

A small crowd had gathered. Some of the ladies had knives to be sharpened, some had scissors, and an old man fom the bottom of the road held a small axe.

"There we is, ma'am. Your old man could shave wiv that now." The rag and bone man held out the chopper to Mum. "That'll be a 'a'penny."

"My bag's on the Morrison, Tim."

"I'll get it, Mum." As Tim ran to the kitchen, he thought about the man. There was something he didn't like about him, the way he looked at you quickly, then looked away.

He found the bag. "Here, Mum."

"Thank you, Tim." She reached into the bag, pulling out the ration books and a small purse, held together by a thick elastic band. She snapped the purse open. "Here," she said, holding out a penny.

The man grumbled and fumbled in his trouser pocket, looking down at the ground. He pulled out a handful of change and with grubby fingers selected a halfpenny from the many in his palm. "There." He thrust it into Mum's hand.

Tim eyed the coin. It looked almost as dirty as the man. Why couldn't he give Mum one of the cleaner ones?

"'Oo's next?" The rag and bone man took a large, bone-handled carving knife. The wheel whirred and sparks flew. "'A'penny." He handed it back. "Next?"

"Where's the old man?" asked Mrs. White as she held out two knives. "Where's Ragsy Thatcher?"

"Sick," said the man, looking away. "Me uncle's sick. Very old and poorly, 'e is. Won't be round no more."

"Shame," said Mrs. Pearson. "I was going to ask him to do something for me."

"What was that, then?"

"Kill one of our birds, a cockerel," said Mrs. Pearson. "I heard he does that."

"I'll do it." The man handed back Mrs. White's knives. "I'll do it when I've finished here."

A short while later, Tim heard a terrible commotion. Mrs. Pearson was screaming. Tim raced down the road and up the Pearson's path to the back garden.

The rag and bone man was in the chicken run, a huge knife in his right hand. He was chasing the birds, wielding the knife like a sword. The chickens fluttered and squawked, darting this way and that in terror.

"Stop it!" shouted Mrs. Pearson. "Stop it, I tell you!"

"Gotcha!" the man shouted. He sliced the head off one of the chickens, and the headless bird ran round and round the run. Finally it fell to the ground, a lifeless heap of bloodied white feathers.

The man wiped his forehead with a piece of cloth, pulling the cap back down over his eyes. "Gotcha." He bent down and grabbed the bird's legs. The other chickens huddled in a corner of the pen, uttering faint cluckings and plaintive warbling sounds.

Mrs. Pearson was crying. "You stupid man."

"'Ere! Wotcha mean?" The man was out of breath.

"That was one of Tom's best layers." Mrs. Pearson

wiped her eyes on her apron. "I asked you to kill one of the cocks."

"Hm." The man stomped out of the run and dropped the dead chicken on the garden path. He threw down the knife. "So that's all the thanks I get."

"Now, tell me again, Tim." Tim was seated at the Morrison in the kitchen. He sipped at his tea. It was very late. Later than he was usually allowed to be up.

"It was different things, Mr. Pearson. First it was his eyes. He kept them covered with his cap, but in the chicken run I saw them, when he wiped his face."

"I noticed them too," said Mrs. Pearson, grimly. "Nasty, mean eyes they were — like a sexton measuring you for a grave, or an undertaker for a coffin."

Tim shivered. Mr. Pearson shook his head. "Now then, dear. You'll scare the lad. Carry on, Tim."

"Well, it was the way he ran. He was small and fat, but he could run really fast."

"Go on," said the air raid warden.

"And then it was the way he spoke, especially when he said 'Gotcha.' And when I thought about it, after he'd gone, I knew who it was."

"Ah." Mr. Pearson nodded. "Good, lad."

"He says it's the same man that chased him

round the graveyard, when we first came here," said Mum. "It's the man that gave him that terrible beating. How could he have the nerve to stand there? He must have known that Tim didn't recognize him, or maybe he didn't recognize Tim."

"I think he did, Mum, in the chicken run. But I don't think he thought I knew. He was so dirty and unshaven, I didn't actually recognize his face, only his eyes."

"Right," said Mr. Pearson. "We'll have him. I'll tell P.C. Harvey. Sounds to me like old Ragsy Thatcher's nephew. He was just a nipper when I was younger. Used to come and stay with old Ragsy, at his scrap yard outside Groombridge. Last time I saw him was just before the war. Quite grown up, he was, with his hair slicked back, wearing a natty, pin-striped suit. Nasty piece of work."

Tim reached for his tea. As he did so, the badge hidden in his hand slipped into his saucer with a clang.

"Hello," said Mr. Pearson. "What's this, then?" He picked up the badge. "Lincoln and Welland. Well I never. Did one of those Canadians give you this?"

Tim shook his head. "I found it in the back field, this afternoon, near where they filled in the trenches."

Mr. Pearson handed back the badge. "Nice souvenir, Tim. You're a lucky lad."

Chapter 15

Normandy

"Mum!" shouted Tim. "It's Grandpa."

The shiny black Morris Eight drove up to the gate. Grandpa George climbed out as Tim ran to the end of the path.

"Steady there, Tim. We don't want any more grazed knees."

"It's okay, Grandpa. My laces are tied. We've been expecting you for ages."

Grandpa nodded. "Had to come a long way round," he said. "There were troops everywhere. Something's up."

"What, Grandpa?"

"I could take a guess, but I'll say nothing." He put his forefinger to his lips. "Walls have ears, you know."

"There aren't any walls here," said Tim.

"Figure of speech," said Grandpa. "You know what I mean. Careless talk costs lives."

Tim nodded. He remembered the posters that warned about saying anything that might help the enemy.

"Grandpa! Grandpa!" Sarah came tearing down the path.

"Careful, young lady. I've just been telling Tim to take it easy." Grandpa hugged Sarah and lifted her high in the air. "My word, you're growing!" He gave her a kiss.

Sarah giggled. "Your moustache is all tickly."

Grandpa gave her another kiss and rubbed his moustache over her cheeks. There were shrieks of laughter.

"Come on," said Grandpa. "Your mother needs help."

Soon they were on their way to Corvuston, luggage in the boot at the back of the car. They were going to live at Grandma and Grandpa's until the new baby came. Close to his chest, Tim held an old shoe-box he'd found in the attic. Inside was the crystal set. He didn't know if it would work at Corvuston, because he hadn't any wire for an aerial. But he wasn't leaving it behind. He felt sleepy in the car. The warm smell of bodies and leather seats, and the hum of the engine weren't making him feel that way. It was the steady purr of the wipers, back and forth. The rain had stopped earlier in the morning, but now it was pouring again. And it was cold, not the usual warm June weather.

"We'll only stay till the baby's born, Dad," Mum was saying.

Grandpa nodded. "Fine, Enid, but we love having you, so don't rush off too soon. Take a rest. You'll need all your strength, with a new little one to take care of."

Mum smiled. "It's difficult these days," she said. "I try to make the food stretch, but it's next to impossible. Do you know, we haven't been able to get potatoes for over a week? And other things are scarce too."

Grandpa nodded. "I was saying to Tim, something's up. We haven't had potatoes either. Can't get them for love or money, and mine aren't ready yet with all this cold wet weather we're having." He steered the car gently round a bend in the narrow country lane, the tires singing on the slick surface of the road.

The hawthorn hedge on either side was thick with new growth. Tim eyed it with interest. It would be good for birdnesting. Maybe he'd find a bullfinch nest at Corvuston. He hadn't found one yet this year.

Grandpa continued. "Something big's going on." He rounded another bend. "Oh, oh. Another diversion."

A military policeman, draped in a rain poncho, stood by a khaki motorcycle. He waved them down. "Morning, all." The soldier peered into the car. "Identity cards, please." As he bent forward, rain water dribbled off the peak of his cap.

Grandpa reached into his coat pocket, and Mum opened her handbag. Out came the bundle of ration books and the purse. Mum snapped off the elastic band and opened Tim's food ration book. Inside was a folded, buff-coloured card.

"Here's yours, Tim." Mum flicked through the books. "And here's yours, Sarah."

Tim wound down the back window on Grandpa's side. Rain came in on his hand. He felt very important. Mum always let them give their own cards.

"Thank you, son." The soldier smiled and handed back the card. It was spotted with rain. He took Sarah's card as she leaned across Tim. "Thank you, luv." He turned to Grandpa. "Can I ask where you're heading for, sir?"

"Corvuston. My daughter-in-law and the children will be staying with us until the new baby arrives."

The soldier smiled. "Right, sir. Thank you." He smiled at Mum. "Good luck, ma'am."

"Thank you." Mum was blushing. "You don't have to tell everyone, Dad."

The policeman laughed and handed back Sarah's card. "Thanks, luv." He leaned on the car. "You'll have to take the long route, by Faridge, I'm afraid, sir."

"That's fine," said Grandpa. "I took this short cut to save petrol, but I've been routed all over the place today. Something big happening?"

The policeman chuckled and shook his head. "You know I can't say anything, sir."

Tim tossed and turned. The bed was really comfortable, but he couldn't stop thinking. A seemingly endless stream of aircraft roared through the night, out and then back. Grandpa was right. Something big was happening.

He awoke to shouting and laughing in the kitchen below. Grandpa was cheering. Feet pounded on the stairs and his bedroom door burst open. It was Sarah.

"You've got to come, Tim! Grandpa says you have to. It's the eight o'clock news. Come on!" She turned and raced back down the corridor.

Tim shook himself awake and rolled out of bed. He needed to go to the toilet.

"Tim!" It was Mum. "You've got to hear this, Tim!"

He plodded down the stairs barefooted, rubbing his eyes. The wireless was blaring in the kitchen. Grandma and Grandpa, Mum and Sarah were huddled round it.

> *"The enemy defensive positions were bombarded by ships of the fleet prior to and during the landing commanded by General Montgomery. Life-sized dummy parachutists were dropped behind the enemy lines. They exploded on impact, throwing the enemy into confusion."*

Grandpa was laughing, rocking back and forth, holding his stomach. "Dummy parachutists! Good old Monty! That's a good one!" He rubbed his hands together. "Yesterday we took Rome, today we're in France."

"This is D-Day! D-Day! That concludes the BBC news."

Grandpa nodded. "Now I know where all the potatoes went. Rations for the troops, God bless 'em."

The next news broadcast was full of the landing. In the House of Commons, Mr. Churchill said the operation had gone "according to plan." Thirty-one thousand airmen in eleven thousand aircraft had flown the missions. And four thousand ships and boats were involved. It was fantastic.

Tim could imagine Bill flying through the night. He hoped Dad had heard the news. Perhaps they'd have news of him soon. He was startled out of his thoughts by the rat-a-tat-tat of the knocker.

Grandpa went to the front door. He returned holding a small, buff-coloured envelope marked OHMS. He carefully slit it open, pulling out a single sheet of paper. As he read, his lips pressed tightly together and the lines of his face seemed to deepen. He breathed in heavily.

"What is it, dear?" Grandma Rose frowned across the table. "I do like to know what's going on."

Grandpa passed the letter to her. She glanced at it and gasped. "Oh, my. Oh —" A tear ran down her cheek, and she passed the letter straight back to Grandpa.

Tim sat looking from one to the other. He knew what OHMS meant — On His Majesty's Service. He saw his mother's face, white, drawn and tense. He felt his chest tighten. Was it about Dad?

Grandpa coughed. "Hrmph." He looked round the table. "It's best you all know. No point in hiding it. I don't think you read it all, did you, Rose?" Grandma shook her head.

Mum put her hand to her mouth, her forehead creased, her eyes holding the wounded look that Tim dreaded.

"It's from Bill's commanding officer," said Grandpa.

Tim felt very cold. He struggled for breath, as if smothered by cloying, black rubber, pressed into cold, damp earth. He swallowed, a hard lump forming at the back of his throat, burning its way slowly and painfully down.

"Now, there is some good news." Grandpa looked round, then at Tim. "Are you all right, Tim?"

Tim nodded, the pain in his chest fading. "Good news, Grandpa?" He swallowed again. "Is Bill okay, Grandpa?"

"I'll read the letter." Grandpa cleared his

throat again. "Hrmph. 'Dear Mr. and Mrs. Athelstan,'" Grandpa continued. "'Flight Lieutenant W. J., Bill, Brewer is a member of my squadron. He gave me your names, among others here in England, to contact in the event that he was shot down. I have to report that on first June, during a night raid, Flight Lieutenant Brewer and his crew were shot down over France. Members of the squadron say they saw the crew bail out. Under the circumstances, no count of survivors could be made, however. The morning after this incident, a Mr. Hawthornthwaite, who lives close to the base, brought me a piece of paper on which were written a set of map coordinates indicating a position near a small town in France called Elbeuf. It had been carried by pigeon. Pigeons are no longer used by the squadron, but I am told by Mr. Hawthornthwaite that Sergeant Roland, the radio operator in the crew, has been carrying a pigeon provided by Mr. Hawthornthwaite. I have compared the writing on the paper returned with the bird. It matches Sergeant Roland's handwriting. Flight Lieutenant Brewer and crew are officially reported as missing, but I have high hopes for their safety. You will understand that this is a personal letter and is not official. I have conveyed the same message to family in Canada. Yours faithfully ...' And then he signs it," said Grandpa.

"Good old Wing Commander Sparklet!" said

Tim. "I was glad when Bill and the crew got a new pigeon."

"So was I," said Sarah. "Good old Wing Commander Sparklet!"

"I agree," said Grandpa. "Wonderful, that bird getting through. We'll pray that they're all safe."

That night, Tim tossed and turned once more. Sparks had set Wing Commander Sparklet free after writing down the map position. That meant that Sparks had parachuted to safety. Bill had his escape pack, and the buttons that were a compass. They had the emergency food, including chocolate. And running through Tim's mind were thoughts of Dad. Rome had been taken. Surely, if Dad had been hiding somewhere, he would now be able to get in touch with the Allied troops?

Chapter 16

Tadpoles and Doodlebugs

"I saw Cherry on the bus today, Mum." Tim took a sip of tea.

"Cherry?"

"You know, Mum. That Canadian soldier who was in the back field last month. The one who knows Bill. They're camped on the heath near here, at Crowborough."

While in Corvuston, Sarah was going to the local village school, but Tim was still at the convent. The journey to Tunbridge Wells was about the same distance as from Medbury.

Tim liked the trip from Corvuston. The bus sped down the hill and weaved its way through the tree-lined lanes into the woods, where the ground was a mass of bluebells. Tim loved bluebells. They covered the earth with a deep blue carpet, from the hedgerow by the road's edge, far into the heart of the woods.

Tim also liked the journey because his friend John from Faridge took the bus too. Just beyond the woods was an old pub, the Rose and Crown, run by John's grandparents. Tim always saved John a seat, up top, at the front of the bus.

"I thought all the Canadian troops were in France," said Mum.

Grandpa shook his head. "Tim's right, there's still a lot on the heath. I hear they're getting restless, want to be where the action is. If only they knew."

"That's what Cherry said." Tim looked at Grandpa. "He said they never get any action, keep missing the boat, getting left behind. He said it was the same in Canada."

"I know what he means," said Grandpa. "But he should count his lucky stars."

"That's right," said Grandma Rose. "That youngster should count his blessings. All men are the same, wanting to dash off to war to get killed. The longer those lads stay on the heath the better off they'll be."

Mum nodded slowly. "Did you tell Cherry about Bill?" she asked Tim.

Tim nodded. "Yes, I did, Mum. Cherry was quiet for a bit, then he laughed. 'Lucky old Bill,' he said."

"What on earth did he mean by that?" said Grandma. "What's lucky about being shot down in enemy territory?"

"He said Bill was always lucky, Grandma. He said he was lucky at school, lucky at hockey, and he said Bill had to be lucky to have a new pigeon, and he would bet anyone that Bill would be safe."

"Pshaw! Betting won't do any good." Grandma shook her head. "Betting? Praying would be better." She busied herself mixing suet and flour. "Dinner tonight will be steamed suet pudding, with gravy from last night's stew."

Tim watched as Grandma mixed the ingredients. Grandma was always going on about praying, these days. He shrugged. He prayed every night for Dad. It didn't seem to have done much good. And now Bill had been shot down!

"Anyway, George," said Grandma, abruptly changing the subject. "If you're going to take the children down to the millpond, you'd better hurry."

"The millpond, Grandpa?" said Tim.

Grandpa George smiled. "I thought you and Sarah would like to go fishing for tadpoles. I've made nets for the two of you."

"They're really good nets, Tim," said Sarah. "Grandpa made them from flour bags."

Tim stared as Grandpa George brought out the two nets. He handed one to Tim. "There you go."

"Thank you, Grandpa." Tim examined the net. The handle was a bean pole. A wire hoop was fastened to the end with butchers' twine. Grandpa had wound the twine tightly and neatly, and Tim couldn't see where the ends were. On the wire hoop was a McDougall's flour bag made from thin cloth. It was perfect. The water would drain out slowly.

"Are you coming, Mum?" asked Tim.

Mum shook her head. She was looking tired.

"Your mother has to rest, Tim," said Grandma. "You should know that by now. She almost lost the baby."

Tim blushed. He'd known that Mum wouldn't come, but somehow he thought he should ask. And sometimes, the way Grandma scolded him for things like that, it was almost as if she thought he made Mum tired. That made him feel really embarrassed.

"Come on, then," said Grandpa. "Let's be off. The two ladies can have a quiet chat without us."

"Amazing!" said Grandpa. "I've never seen anything like it."

The shore was almost completely covered with tiny frogs, jumping here and there, testing their new legs. Fishing for tadpoles was out.

Grandpa scratched his head. "It's been so cold this year, I didn't think we'd have any trouble getting a tad or two. Thought they'd still be in the water."

Tim swung his jam jar by the string handle. "Maybe if we got down to the water there might still be some?"

"Can't do it, lad." Grandpa shook his head. "We'd kill hundreds of these little blighters before we got there. Don't want to do that, now, do we?"

Tim shook his head.

"I don't want to kill any," said Sarah. "They're so tiny and sweet."

"Well, we're too late for tads," said Grandpa, "but this is a sight you probably won't see again. I never have. It's incredible!" He took a step back. "Oops! Can't walk that way, either."

The tiny frogs seemed to be attracted to Grandpa's feet. He couldn't help crushing a few. As he retraced his steps they leapt onto the path, landing beneath his boots.

Sarah was shivering.

"What's the matter, Sarah? You're not getting a cold, are you?"

"No, Grandpa." Sarah shook her head. "They look like tiny men, Grandpa, tiny, dead men."

Tim shivered too. He looked down at the crushed, lifeless bodies, sprawled on the footpath. Sarah was right. They did look like miniature men. He looked round. There were more bodies on the path behind them, small, green, khaki-coloured bodies. He hadn't realized that they'd trodden on so many. He felt as if he was looking down from the sky, flying above a battlefield, seeing the destruction. Sarah screamed, bringing him back down to earth.

"Go away!" Sarah was waving her arms wildly. "Go away, you horrible beasts!" Crows were swooping down among the tiny frogs.

"It won't do any good, Sarah," said Grandpa. "As soon as we're gone, they'll be back."

"But we've got to stop them." Sarah turned and swung her net at a diving crow. It cawed defiantly as it veered away. Sarah stepped on more baby frogs. She started to cry.

Grandpa bent down and lifted her in his arms. He shook his head. "They're just trying to feed their families." He held Sarah close. "I'm sorry, love."

Sarah sobbed. "Well, I don't think it's very nice of them."

"It's only like a blackbird or a thrush eating worms," said Tim. Maybe that explanation would help.

"No, it's not." Sarah glared at him from red-rimmed eyes. She sniffed.

Tim tried again. He thought of last night's dinner. "You liked the stew we had yesterday, didn't you, Sarah? It's like eating stew."

"It's not the same." Sarah stared down at him. "Worms are not babies, and stew isn't babies." She sniffed again. "Those baby frogs are babies."

"Hrmph." Tim looked at his grandfather. He was slowly shaking his head.

Tim couldn't stop thinking about the late afternoon outing as he went to sleep that night. He snuggled down into bed and pulled the pillow up round his ears. It was really cold for June. At supper, Grandma had tried to explain to Sarah that French people ate frogs' legs. That only made things worse. Sarah wanted to know why everyone was fighting to get France back, if the people were cruel and ate frogs. Tim wondered what frogs' legs tasted like. He wondered if the Germans in France ate them. Grandma said she'd heard that frogs tasted like chicken. Tim's eyelids began to feel heavy. Perhaps Bill was eating frogs.

He'd forgotten to say his prayers. He climbed out of bed and knelt on the floor. He didn't know what to say anymore. He'd prayed so often, but nothing happened. He couldn't think. There was the steady drone of bombers overhead. They were flying south to cross the Channel. It had been the same every night for days. He climbed back into bed. Maybe he'd think what to say tomorrow night. He lay listening to the drone of engines high in the night sky. And the sound of planes mingled with the cawing of crows as they dived among the frogs. He turned restlessly in sleep.

Tim sat bolt upright in bed. Something had wakened him. What was it? Then he heard the eerie, moaning wail of the air-raid siren as it rose and fell. It sent shudders down his spine. Grandpa had said that the raids were long over.

The troops had landed in France and the last bomb around Corvuston had been in March, two and a half months ago, and that had only been from a stray night raider.

In the distance, behind the wail of the siren, was a deep, sinister hum. But it didn't sound like a bomber, or a fighter. The noise grew louder, an ugly, clattering, menacing sound, mixing with the high-pitched wail of the siren.

Tim jumped out of bed and rushed to the window. The noise was now deafening, a hideous rattle. He flung back the curtains and the blackout. Outlined against the night sky was a sinister black cross, a flaming wake of fire trailing behind it, lighting the low clouds.

Downstairs, in the front hall, the clock struck four. The noise from the sky grew deafening as the hideous thing passed overhead. The wail of the siren rose and fell. Doors banged and there were footsteps in the hall.

"What on earth was that?" Mum shouted.

"It's all right, Enid," said Grandma. Tim heard her hurry past his door. "Whatever it was, it's gone over."

"Sounded like some poor blighter in trouble," said Grandpa. "Why's the siren sounding?" He opened Tim's door. "Are you awake, Tim? Where —? Oh, you're over there. Get away from the window!"

"Sorry, Grandpa." Tim quickly pulled the blackout to and shut the curtains. "I saw it,

Grandpa. It was on fire, and —"

There was crying down the hall. It was Sarah.

"Damn!" said Grandpa. He banged his clenched fist on the door post. "Damn, damn, damn. I thought this nonsense was long over."

The siren continued its insistent wail.

"Don't you think we'd better get down to the shelter, George?" said Grandma. "That siren hasn't stopped."

"You're right, dear." He shook his head. "Dressing gowns on, everyone, and down to the shelter. I wonder what the time is?"

"It's four o'clock, Grandpa. I heard the clock in the hall downstairs."

Grandpa George sighed. "Get your dressing gown, Tim. Come on, lad." He called down the hall again. "In the shelter. Come on." He grumbled as he trundled down the stairs ahead of Tim. "Good excuse to put the kettle on for a cuppa, I suppose. We'll not get back to sleep, packed in the Morrison like sardines. Hurry, now!"

"Can I have one, Grandpa?"

"Have one what, Tim?"

"Cup of tea, Grandpa."

"Of course, Tim. And maybe, just maybe, I can find some biscuits."

The sirens wailed. Up and down, up and down.

Chapter 17

L-for-Lucky Lancaster

"How long will Mummy have to stay in the hospital?" asked Sarah.

"It's not a hospital, dear, it's a nursing home." Grandma Rose poured tea. "She must stay there until the baby comes. Since that first buzz-bomb, Mummy hasn't been well. She has to rest. If she doesn't, she could lose the baby."

"Who would find it?" asked Sarah.

"What, dear?"

"Who would find the baby if Mummy lost it? Would they give it back?"

Tim burst out laughing. He didn't know much about babies, but he did know losing a baby meant having it die. Grandma didn't mean Mum would lose it like losing a book or something. Grandma Rose stared at him across the table, a stern look on her face.

"Hrmph. Time to explain that another day,"

said Grandpa. "Sarah? More treacle?" He sipped his tea.

"Yes, please, Grandpa."

Tim was glad that Grandpa had broken the tension. He didn't mean to laugh at Sarah. It was just that she said funny things sometimes.

Grandpa dipped the spoon in the treacle, turning it slowly. It came out laden with golden syrup. As he passed it to Sarah, a drip fell, running slowly down the side of the tin, over the golden lion's head. Grandpa smiled. "Can't let him have that." He wiped it off with the tip of his finger. The smile disappeared and he took a sip of tea. "We'll sleep in the Morrison tonight. Wretched buzz-bombs."

"They called them flying-bombs on the wireless, today, dear," said Grandma.

"That's right," said Grandpa. "I heard that."

"I call them dragons," said Sarah.

Tim stared at his sister. What was she talking about? "Why do you call them dragons?"

"Because they're horrible and nasty, and they have tails of flame." Sarah sounded pleased with herself.

"Mm. That's very good, dear," said Grandma Rose.

"But dragons don't have tails of flame," said Tim, scornfully. "They have tongues — well — they breathe fire."

Sarah's smile disappeared, and tears welled up in her eyes. Grandma Rose looked angry. "It doesn't matter if they have tails of flame, or tongues or whatever." Her voice had a sharp edge to it. "I can see what Sarah means."

Tim shrugged. Maybe they did look like dragons to Sarah. "We spent most of the day under our desks," he said. He looked round. No one seemed interested. "We were under them before the sirens went."

Grandpa looked across at him. "Why did you take cover before the alert sounded, Tim?"

"One of the older nuns was up on the roof, with a whistle and a bell."

"In all this rain?" said Grandma.

Tim nodded. "She had a huge umbrella. She came down when the rain and hail started. She's our spotter."

"What was she doing up there?" Sarah looked puzzled.

"She looks for buzz-bombs," said Tim. "When she sees one, she blows the whistle and rings the bell. Then the other nuns ring their bells and we get under our desks. There were bells ringing all day."

"I don't like you going to Tunbridge Wells," said Grandma. "But your mother doesn't want you to miss any more school." She shook her head. "And I don't like your mother being at the nursing home, all by herself."

"But there are lots of ladies there, Grandma," said Sarah.

"What I mean, dear, is that we're not all together. Tim is miles away, Mummy isn't here." Grandma opened the newspaper. "And then we get news like this." She pointed to the newspaper. "Hospitals being bombed!" Grandma frowned. "And people are leaving London again. These bombs are evil, like that man, Hitler. And I heard in the village this morning that some bombs might carry poison gas."

Tim's chest tightened. Gas! The bread and treacle stuck in his throat and he almost choked.

Grandpa nodded slowly. "I heard that when I went for the paper. I want everyone in the shelter tonight. And get out the gas masks." He looked across the table-top of the Morrison. "I'll help you with yours, Sarah."

Tim could feel the sweat running down his back. He looked at the windows where rain thudded, splattering on the glass. The strips of paper, plastered on the windows to prevent a mass of jagged splinters flying in if a bomb hit, were old and faded. Everything looked heavy, damp and dismal. He shuddered. He didn't want any more tea. Then he looked at Sarah. She'd never had to wear a proper mask. But there was fear in her eyes. And the memory flooded back — baby Sarah, her hair matted with mud, clinging to Mum, as they stood by the shattered shelter, staring wide-eyed at the burning house and then at Tim's mask. He felt prickles of fear in his neck.

He swallowed, and the bread and treacle moved slowly down, a solid, hard lump.

"Can I go up to my room, Grandma?" he whispered.

"Can't you finish that sandwich?" Grandma looked at him in surprise. "My word, you do look pale. Aren't you feeling well?"

Tim shook his head. "I'll lie down for a while."

Grandpa leaned over and felt Tim's forehead. "Mm. No temperature. Have a nap," he said cheerily. "You'll feel much better. Then we'll get this old shelter organized."

Tim didn't go to sleep. He knelt on the floor and reached under the bed. There it was, the hated cardboard box. He'd almost left it at Medbury, but Mum had checked all their things and had thrown it into the boot of the Morris Eight. He pulled. The string was caught. He stretched out on the floor and reached under the bed. It wasn't caught on the springs. It was over the shoe-box containing the crystal set. He pulled out both boxes and sighed. He hadn't been able to set up an aerial. But seeing the crystal set reminded him of what Bill had said:

"You'll feel just like a radio operator up there in big old L-for-Lucky Lancaster."

He hesitated for a moment and then opened the shoe-box. He couldn't use the crystal set, but he could use the earphones and pretend he was a pilot, like Bill, in command on a bombing raid. He took out the headset. Then, hesitating again, he opened the other box. The warm, cloying smell of rubber filled his nostrils. He could taste it. He felt his stomach heave. Then he remembered the look in Sarah's eyes.

"Sometimes, especially when you're in charge, you have to do things you don't want to, or maybe don't like, to help others."

Tim nodded slowly, remembering Bill's words when he'd given him the penny Spitfire. Bill had wanted the bomber's tour to be over. "See you in a month," Bill had said. And Tim remembered his Dad's words, almost a year ago:

"Look after Mummy and Sarah for me, Tim."

He lifted out the mask. He had to help Sarah. Mum was in the nursing home. He was in charge. "L-for-Lucky Lancaster," he whispered. "L-for-Lucky Lancaster," he said, louder. Slowly he lifted the mask toward his face. The heavy, pungent, sweaty smell of the rubber was overpowering. He thought of Bill at the controls of the bomber, of Sparks listening to the whistles and crackles in the earphones, of Wing Commander Sparklet in his cage beside Sparks. "L-for-Lucky Lancaster," Tim repeated. Then, taking an enormous gulp of air, he pulled on the mask.

The rubber clung to his face and the thick, black bands pulled at his hair. "L-for-Lucky Lancaster." His voice was muffled. He sucked in air. He could breathe! He picked up the headset and put it on, the earpieces fitting snugly. There was no noise, no crackling or whistling, but Tim felt excitement mounting inside him. "L-for-Lucky Lancaster. This is L-for-Lucky Lancaster." He breathed in deeply. "This is L-for-Lucky Lancaster."

"Whatever are you doing, Tim?" It was Grandma. She stood at the bedroom door, staring at him. "We've been calling you. We have to get the shelter ready."

Tim looked up through the eyepiece of the mask. He was smiling.

Rain beat down outside. Tim knew there was lightning, but they couldn't see it through the blackout. Thunder cracked and roared. He felt cosy in the shelter.

"Now, Sarah, you do it like this."

Sarah shrank back from the black rubber mask.

"I'll show her, Grandpa." Tim took his gas mask out of the box. His sister looked at him in surprise. "You take yours, Sarah. Right, now do exactly what I do."

Tim bent his head forward, slowly lifting the mask toward his face. It still smelled awful. "L-for-Lucky Lancaster," he said.

"Why are you saying that?" asked Sarah.

"Because of Bill," said Tim. "I'm pretending to be a bomber pilot putting on my oxygen mask. You do it!"

Grandpa George nodded approvingly. "By

golly," he said, "we'll not let Hitler's dragons beat us, will we, Sarah?"

Sarah smiled and shook her head. "L-for-Lucky," she said.

"Lancaster," said Tim. "L-for-Lucky Lancaster." He pulled on his mask. "This is L-for-Lucky Lancaster."

His muffled voice was drowned by the wail of the siren, rising shrilly above the rain. Then, moments later, he heard a harsh, menacing growl in the distance, increasing to a staccato roar, shaking the house, making the cups on top of the Morrison jump and rattle.

"If my favourite cup gets broken, I'll be fighting mad," shouted Grandpa, above the din.

The buzz-bomb seemed to be right over the house, the grating, sinister, pulsing sound, beating, beating, beating down. Tim crouched in his corner, against the wire mesh, pressing himself into the blankets. His breathing was harsh in the mask. He pulled it off. Then he felt a small hand reach into his own. Sarah pressed herself close, and he put his arm round her shoulder.

The dreadful noise stopped. There was an eerie, terrifying silence. The engine had cut out. It was coming down.

Tim began to count, silently, as they did at school: One-and, two-and, three-and, four —

Grandpa roared. "Damn! Hold onto one another!" Tim felt the old man's arms reach out, round him and Sarah. He could smell the sweet smell of lavender as Grandma pressed close. Grandma's heart was thudding, louder than his own. He could feel it.

The rain beat down, drumming a tattoo on the roof. Then, with a splutter, the engine roared into life. The cups on the Morrison bounced and clattered. The roar began to fade, and then there was silence again.

Tim began to count: One-and, two-and, three-and ... ten-and, eleven —

There was an enormous explosion. The house shook. A cup fell, splintering on the kitchen floor.

"Damn!" roared Grandpa George. "My favourite cup!"

Chapter 18

Dragons in the Sky

There was no time to examine the site of the bomb that morning. Tim had to go to school. Grandma was all for him staying home, but Grandpa George said that Hitler had disrupted enough, without ruining Tim's education.

On his way to the bus stop, Tim met the milkman. "Do you know where the bomb crashed?" Tim asked.

"Down by the millpond, I'm told. Maybe in it."

Tim remembered the thousands of young frogs. Grandpa had been right. They'd never see that sight again.

The dark green Maidstone and District doubledecker bus gathered speed as it roared down the slope into the shadow of the tree-lined hollow. Toiling up the narrow lane on the far side, it slowed down, almost grinding its way to the top. There were still a few bluebells in the woods, but not the dense carpet of a few weeks ago. The bus emerged from the trees into bright sunlight.

Tim sat alone, up top, in the front. There was nobody else up there today. He could see far ahead, across the field, where sheep grazed contentedly while their lambs gambolled and frolicked. In the distance, round the bend, was the Rose and Crown, where his friend John lived. A small group of people stood at the bus stop outside the pub. They seemed to be staring up at the sky. One of the tiny figures was pointing. It looked like John.

In the field, the sheep and lambs started to scatter, some in a tight bunch, others running aimlessly this way and that. A flock of crows suddenly rose into the air, a seething cloud of black wings, heading up and over the bus. The knot of people at the bus stop disappeared into the pub.

Then, above the lazy rumble of the engine, Tim heard a dreadful throbbing, low-level roar, the raucous rattle of a doodlebug. No wonder the noise was so loud — there wasn't just one flying-bomb, there were three, heading across the distant fields. With their pointed noses and squat, square-ended wings, they looked like huge black daggers speeding straight for him, their tails of flame burning a deadly course toward the bus.

Above the menacing rattle of the flying-bombs, Tim heard the engine of the bus roar into life, and with a jerk, the doubledecker picked up speed, slowly at first and then faster, careering at full throttle down the narrow country road.

There was a shout. "Get down here, luv!"

The clippie's voice barely penetrated Tim's thoughts as he stared, mesmerized by the sight of the three doodlebugs. The flame behind the one in the middle was no longer burning, and as Tim watched, it began to fall, nose first, but veering slightly to one side. The bus seemed to be a magnet as the deadly flying-bomb followed it round the bend in the road. The bus swayed dangerously, and Tim fell.

"Please, luv!" screamed the clippie. "Get down here!"

The fall had startled Tim. The deadly drone of the two flying-bombs was receding, but the dreadful quiet of the third was a sinister threat. He couldn't see it. Where was it? How many seconds was it since the engine had cut out? He raced down the aisle and reached the top of the stairs, clinging onto the rail. As he did so, the sun was blotted from the rear window by a hideous black shape. Tim stared, transfixed. It was only momentary, but for that short time the monster appeared to be upon him.

There was a screeching of brakes. Tim fell, tumbling headfirst down the stairs. The whole world seemed to erupt, a fiery, red, hellish glow. The last thing Tim remembered, before hitting his head, was swallowing thick, black, gritty dust and acrid smoke.

"Poor little mite. He's covered in blood."

Tim opened his eyes. He struggled to sit up. A hand pushed him firmly, yet gently, back.

"There, there, lad. Lie back. We've sent for help."

Tim looked up at the lady in the ATS uniform. Her eyes were kind. She stroked his forehead and then looked at her fingers. Tim looked too — they were covered in blood. His eyes widened in horror. He must be injured. But he didn't feel injured. Suppose he was paralysed!

"We couldn't help anyone else on the bus." The lady shook her head. "The blast from the pub tore through it. You were saved because you were in the stairwell."

"The conductor," said Tim. "She ..."

The ATS lady shook her head and looked away.

Tim closed his eyes. He moved his fingers, then his hands. He could feel them and they didn't hurt. He wiggled his toes in his boots and bent his knees. Nothing was hurting except his head, and that wasn't at the front, where the blood was, it was at the back. He opened his eyes. The ATS lady was a short way away, talking to some soldiers. Tim sat up. He didn't hurt anywhere except his head, but that hurt like fury.

Tim looked round. He was lying on the grass verge, near a hedge. But the hedge was bare of leaves, as if it was mid-winter. The grass was short and brown. He pushed himself up and struggled to his feet.

"Hey!" One of the soldiers ran toward him.

"I'm all right," said Tim. "Honestly I am." He reached into his pocket. It felt sticky and wet. He looked down. The bottom of his jacket was a deep red, shiny in places, dark, almost maroon in others. He drew back his hand in horror.

He looked round. Close by, on the verge, was the body of the clippie. A soldier was covering her with a coat. Her head was at a funny angle, one leg doubled beneath her. Half her clothes were gone. The bus driver was hanging out of a passenger window, his uniform in shreds. The sun glinted on the ragged edges of torn metal, the front of the bus ripped open, the top gone, lying in the field. There was glass everywhere, and a terrible smell. Tim started to shiver. The passengers downstairs sat still and unmoving in twisted metal seats. Tim felt dizzy and his stomach heaved.

"Come away, lad," said the soldier. He took hold of Tim's hand. "Come away." He caught Tim as he swayed. "Are you sure you're all right?"

Tim nodded. He stepped fearfully past the shrouded body of the conductor. He'd seen her every morning on the run from Corvuston to Tunbridge Wells. He didn't look at the driver. Then he saw the pub where John lived with his grandparents. Flames licked at the crumbling brick and stone. The inn sign hung by one small piece of chain, the remains of the shattered pole stuck in the broken, leafless branches of an uprooted tree. Two soldiers carried out a small, limp figure. Tim fainted.

"Murderers!" shouted Grandma Rose. "Murderers!"

It was three days since the doodlebug had killed John and his grandparents. They had been in the shelter in a corner of the cellar at the Rose and Crown. Grandma had heard that the blast from the bomb had sucked all the air from the building, and they'd died in just one, short second, huddled together.

Tim couldn't understand why Grandma was shouting. She'd cried when he'd been brought home that day, and she'd cried when she learned about the pub. She'd known John's family all her life. She'd talked to Grandpa, in hushed tones, when she didn't think he and Sarah were around. But today she'd seemed better. Now this.

"Murdering swine!" Grandma threw down the wiping-up cloth and glared at Grandpa George. "I can't believe it."

Grandpa shook his head. "The Gestapo are capable of anything," he said.

Tim was puzzled. He hadn't seen anything in the Sunday Express yesterday, and Grandpa hadn't fetched today's paper. Maybe Grandma meant that report about bombs hitting two more hospitals. At one of them, seven patients had been killed. The other hospital was full of people injured in other flying-bomb attacks. Some of them were children. He wondered whether the King and Queen had visited those children before the bombs hit. Perhaps the King had given them medals, as he'd done for some children in Normandy two weeks before. Grandma said the King shouldn't go to France as he might get killed, but Grandpa said it was exactly what the troops needed, seeing the King over there with them.

Maybe Grandma was upset about the fighting in the streets of Copenhagen. That had been reported on the back page of the Sunday paper. It said that fifteen thousand Danish people were fighting. Then they were machine-gunned, by planes swooping down, time after time, sweeping the streets with a hail of bullets.

But the report that had interested Tim the most was about a fighter pilot, "Johnny" Johnson. Tim had read it three times. Johnny had shot down his thirty-third plane and beaten the record of thirty-two, set by another pilot, named "Sailor" Milan, in the Battle of Britain. And "Johnny" Johnson led a Canadian fighter group before he went on leave. When his leave finished, they'd asked to have him back to lead their Spitfire squadron again. That's what Bill wanted to do, fly Spitfires.

"All those young pilots murdered in cold blood," said Grandma. "It's criminal murder."

"Pilots murdered, Grandma? Where?"

"Forty-seven flying officers who escaped from a prisoner of war camp, Tim. Stalag Luft Three, or something like that, they called it. There were twenty-five British officers, six Canadians and —"

Tim gasped. His heart thudded. Suppose ...

But Grandma was shaking her head. "I can see what you're thinking," she said. "Don't worry. This happened back in March, but we've only just been told about it. Mr. Eden spoke about it on the news, a few minutes before you came down. I remember now. It was Stalag Luft Three. That's what he called it."

Tim nodded slowly. "They murdered them?" he whispered.

"Hrmph." Grandpa cleared his throat. "Not all of them, Tim. Mr. Eden said that some of them are still free — fourteen or fifteen, I think. And some of them were captured and are back in the camp. But ..." He pressed his lips together and breathed in deeply, shaking his head slowly. "The Nazis, the Gestapo ... well, they shot the rest. Rounded them up and shot them. Forty-seven fine young men doing their duty."

Tim still wanted to be sure. "Where's that camp you said, Grandma?"

Grandma sighed. "We're told it's near Dresden, Tim. That's what makes it seem all the more terrible."

"Why?"

Grandma sighed again. "It's a city where they make the most beautiful china. We have some. That lovely little figurine on the shelf at the top of the stairs, that's Dresden. And to think that where such beauty is created, such evil can be done."

The room was silent. Tim was glad that the murders had happened three months ago, and a long way from where they thought Bill was, but he felt guilty, thinking that. It meant that Bill couldn't have been there, even if he'd been captured by now. But all those other young pilots were dead. A picture of the clippie and the bus driver flashed through his mind. He shuddered.

Grandpa pushed back his chair. "Well, we have plenty of time for a cuppa, before going to visit your mother. I'll put the kettle on, Grandma will wake Sarah, you set the cups, Tim, and ..." He looked at Grandma. She was shaking her head. "Ah." Grandpa sighed. "No biscuits? Hrmph." Grandpa growled. "Running out of everything. I love a biscuit with my tea."

"What about your secret supplier, Grandpa?"

"Out of everything, lad. Out of everything."

The nursing home smelled strongly of soap and disinfectant. No wonder Sarah kept calling it a hospital. A nurse came hurrying across the white-tiled floor.

"How did you know?" she said.

"Know?" said Grandpa. "Know what?"

"You mean, you don't know?" The nurse spread her arms, a broad smile on her face.

"The baby?" said Grandma. "Enid's had the baby, hasn't she?"

The nurse nodded eagerly. "Last night, during the raid. Beautiful baby. Came at —"

"But what is it?" interrupted Grandpa.

Tim was glad Grandpa had asked. He wanted to know too. He still wasn't sure how he felt about the idea of a baby brother. He wouldn't be able to play for a long time, and —

"Is Mummy's baby a girl?" asked Sarah.

The nurse smiled. Then she nodded. "Lovely fair hair, just like you and your brother. Beautiful hands. But don't let's stand here. Come on." She bustled away down the hall.

"Now," said Mum. "What day do you want baby Jane to have as her birthday, Sunday or Monday?" She looked down into the cot beside the bed.

"What do you mean, Mum?" Tim stared at his new sister. She was so tiny, and her fair hair was very thin. He wasn't sure that he'd call her beautiful.

"Well, Tim," Mum was saying, "the doctor said that, as she was born just seconds after midnight, she could have her birthday on Monday."

"Hrmph." Grandpa coughed. "But if she came after midnight, Enid, then that's it. She was born on Monday."

Tim nodded. Grandpa was right. After midnight last night it was Monday. If you were born on Monday, then that was when you were born. He looked back at the cot. Baby Jane was sleeping.

Mum smiled. "But, as Dr. Hume says, if there wasn't a war on, we wouldn't have double daylight-saving time. The clocks wouldn't be two hours ahead, only one."

"Ah. I see." Grandma smiled. "If the clocks were only one hour ahead then baby Jane would have been born on Sunday."

"That's right." Mum nodded. "So what shall we do? The doctor will write up the birth certificate either way."

"Bags I, Sunday," said Tim.

"Why?" said Grandpa. "'Monday's child is fair of face,' and you couldn't have a more beautiful sister."

Tim looked into the cot. He still didn't think that baby Jane was beautiful, but he had something more important on his mind. "I don't want Hitler making my sister have a different birthday," he said.

"Right," said Grandpa. "Good thinking, lad. What do you say, Sarah?"

"I bags Sunday, too, Grandpa — like Tim."

“That’s it then.” Grandpa rubbed his hands together and smiled. “Sunday it is.”

“Wait, now, George.” Grandma was shaking her head. “I think Enid has to make the final decision.”

“Hrmph.” Grandpa coughed. “Sorry, Enid.” He looked down at his hands.

Mum laughed. It was the happiest laugh Tim had heard from her in ages. “Sunday,” she said. “Of course it has to be Sunday. We’ll not let Hitler tell us what to do, will we?”

Chapter 19

Cherry

"Terrible thing, that," said Grandpa.

"What, dear?" Grandma Rose looked up from her darning. She was repairing holes in the heels of Tim's socks. The grey darning wool was not the same colour as the socks, but no one would see them inside his boots.

"Up on the heath," said Grandpa. "That doodlebug that came down yesterday evening hit the Canadian troops' camp. Quite a few killed, I hear."

"What?" shouted Tim. "You mean a doodlebug hit the camp where Cherry is?"

"Cherry? Who's Cherry?"

"You remember, Grandpa. I told you about the Canadian soldiers in the back field at Medbury. Cherry's Bill's friend."

"Yes. I do remember." Grandpa nodded. "As I understand it, the wretched thing hit the mess tent or the kitchen, I'm not sure which. It was around dinner time."

Tim couldn't believe it. He felt the hard metal of the cap badge in his pocket. He had to find out if Bill's friend was all right. "Grandpa. We have to go up there."

"We can't do that, Tim."

"But we have to, Grandpa. Cherry is Bill's friend from school." As he said this, Tim felt a lump in his throat. Only days ago, his own best friend, John, had been killed by a doodlebug. He wasn't going to cry. He struggled on. "We have to, Grandpa, it's ..."

"It's like John being dead, isn't it, Tim?"

Tim glared at his sister. Tears began to well up and he quickly looked away. Why did Sarah have to say that?

"Ah." Grandma was nodding. "I think you might try, don't you, George?"

"Well." Grandpa pursed his lips and blew out slowly, through his grey moustache. "I'll try," he said.

"Can I come, Grandpa? I won't get in the way, I promise."

"Me too, Grandpa?" Sarah had that pleading look in her eyes. "I promise, too."

Tim glared at his sister again. Why did she always have to butt in? He saw the worried look on Sarah's face. She knew he was angry. He shook his head. He'd been getting more and more annoyed with Sarah since they'd come to Corvuston. Maybe it was because she was always asking questions. Usually they were questions he wanted to ask but felt silly doing so. He sighed. She wasn't a bad sister, really. She did stick up for him.

"I don't mind if Sarah comes, Grandpa. I'll look after her."

Sarah smiled happily.

"Right." Grandpa looked from one to the other. "We'll go then. But it's a fair walk — probably three quarters of an hour to get there, and then the same back, of course. It's quite a bit further than the old mill pond."

The smile faded from Sarah's face. "Aren't we going in the car?" she said.

Grandpa shook his head. "No. I can't use the petrol. I have to save it."

"Oh." Sarah looked at Grandma Rose. "I'll stay and help Grandma," she said.

Grandma smiled. "Thank you, dear. I'm sure we can find lots of things to do."

As Tim sat on the step at the back door, tying the laces on his boots, he wondered if Sarah had said she'd stay because she'd seen the look on his face, or because of the walk. Grandma said he had quite a scowl, like his father had as a boy. She said she could read his face like a book.

Sarah came to the door. "I don't mind staying with Grandma," she said.

Tim nodded. "I don't mind if you come, really I don't." He saw the look of disbelief on Sarah's face. "Honestly, Sarah. I do mean it. I really don't mind."

Sarah shook her head. "It's too far. Grandpa says it's up by that place where he used to play golf before the soldiers came. Grandma says you won't be home until dinner."

It was a long walk, but Tim enjoyed it. It was the first time Grandpa had really spoken to him about Dad.

"Young Will and I used to walk up here, when he was a boy," said Grandpa. "Uncle Richard and young Raymond didn't come much. They weren't interested in birds' eggs like your dad was. While I played golf, your dad would go nesting in the woods. I've still got his collection in the garage."

"Can I see them, Grandpa?"

Grandpa nodded. "I know Will would like that." He nodded again. "There's one egg he's particularly proud of."

"What is it, Grandpa?"

"It's a Guillemot egg. I remember the day he got it, at Eastbourne, up at Beachy Head."

Tim remembered the chalk cliffs at Beachy Head. They were high. He'd looked over once, watching the sea pound the base of the chalk as if it wanted to tear the cliffs down.

Grandpa continued. "Grandma and I were visiting Grandpa Cecil and Grandma Maude. Cecil had been a great egg collector as a boy. He'd shown Will his collection quite a few times, but he didn't have a Guillemot egg." He smiled. "Anyway, your father, Uncle Raymond and Auntie Beatrice went for a walk on the Downs. About an hour after they'd left, Bea came tearing into the house, screaming that Will was going to fall. He'd climbed down to a nest and was having trouble getting back up. Cecil got out his Standard Twelve and we drove like fury to Beachy Head. Did I tan Will's behind!" Grandpa breathed in deeply. "I remember that," he said quietly. "It's a wonder the egg survived. Grandma was all for throwing it into the sea. Cecil stopped her."

They were approaching the entrance to the camp. A sentry came to attention and marched forward two paces. There were CANADA flashes on his shoulders. "This is a military camp, sir." His voice had that same lazy drawl that Tim associated with Bill.

Grandpa nodded. "Yes, son. I know that." He rested his hand on Tim's shoulder. "But you see, my grandson here knows someone in your regiment, and after that terrible ..."

Tim looked at the soldier. He hadn't seen him in the back field at Medbury. He peered through the mass of barbed wire. Another figure was approaching. He had three stripes on his arm.

The sergeant marched up smartly, his boots crunching on the gravel pathway. "Can I help?"

"I want to know about Cherry," said Tim, quickly. "Is he all right?"

"Cherry?" The sergeant looked puzzled.

"B Platoon, I think, Sarge," said the sentry. "I don't know if ..."

"Yes." The sergeant held up his hand. "I see."

"The gentleman says the boy knows him."

"I do." Tim looked anxiously from one to the other. "I live at Medbury. You camped there, remember?"

"Medbury? That's a long way from here." The sergeant looked up the road. "I ..."

Grandpa George coughed. "Perhaps I'd better explain. We didn't come from Medbury today. The boy's staying with us at Corvuston, while my daughter-in-law is in the nursing home."

"Mum's just had a baby," said Tim. "She was born on Sunday, not Monday. We're not letting Hitler beat us."

"Hrmph." Grandpa coughed again. "What he means is ..." Grandpa shook his head. "I'd have to go through the whole thing for you to understand."

The sergeant smiled. "I can't wait to hear the end of this one." He looked down at Tim. "We're not going to let Hitler beat us, either. We're gonna strike him out. But step inside for a minute." He ushered Tim and Grandpa through the gap in the barbed wire.

Grandpa looked awkward. "Look ... I'm sorry about what happened yesterday."

The sergeant nodded slowly. "Those poor guys. All they wanted was to get over to France, to fight the Hun. That's what we've trained for. So what happens? Hitler hits us while we're sitting here like a bunch of civvies."

Grandpa coughed. "Hrmph."

"Oh, gee! I'm sorry, sir. No offence. It's just that we always seem to be behind the eight ball. Never get to see any action."

"Don't apologize, Sergeant." Grandpa stroked his moustache. "I felt the same way when I was your age. I wasn't always a civilian, you know."

"No, sir. Look, can I get you a cup of tea, some cookies?"

"Cookies?" Grandpa looked confused.

"Biscuits, Grandpa. That's what they call them."

"Ah." Grandpa smiled. "We wouldn't say no to a cuppa and a biscuit, now would we?"

Tim shook his head. He turned to the sergeant. "Grandpa loves a biscuit with his tea, and we haven't got any."

The sergeant winked. "I think I can fix that. Quick march!"

As they walked into the camp Tim looked round, searching the faces of the Canadian soldiers. He couldn't see anyone he remembered from Medbury. The camp was bustling with activity. A jeep came roaring past, screeching to a halt in front of a tent.

"Slow down a bit!" shouted the sergeant as a soldier jumped out. The man turned and Tim yelled:

"Cherry! Grandpa! It's Cherry!"

The soldier hesitated, turned and waved, then ran inside the tent.

"So that's Cherry." The sergeant smiled. "That wasn't too hard." He nodded. "He must have some urgent dispatches. I'll tell him to join us in a minute. Wait here." He marched off and entered the tent.

Tim looked round. There were vehicles everywhere — huge troop-carrying Bedford lorries, bren gun carriers, armoured cars, jeeps and motorcycles, all painted with dull khaki paint and camouflage markings. They had patches covering the signs that would identify the unit they belonged to.

Tim looked at Grandpa, and Grandpa nodded. Something's up, thought Tim. The Canadians were going to move out soon, he was sure of it.

Near where they stood was a pile of rubbish. Something caught Tim's eye. It was a roll of thin wire, insulated with turns of cotton. It was like the wire Bill had brought for the aerial for the crystal set. Tim wandered over and was feeling the wire when the sergeant returned.

"The guy you call Cherry will be out in minute." He smiled at Tim. "What's so interesting about that garbage?" he asked.

"It would make a super aerial for my wireless," said Tim. "For my crystal set."

"Crystal set?" The sergeant smiled. "Gee. That

takes me back a year or two. You need some wire? Take it."

Tim couldn't believe his ears. "You mean I can have some?"

"Sure thing. Take the lot if you want. It'll only be dumped. Here, don't be shy." The sergeant pulled the roll of wire from the heap and handed it to Tim. It was heavy.

Tim sat on his bed. Yesterday had been an exciting day at the Canadian troops' camp.

Grandpa had come home by jeep. On his lap were two very large tins of cookies; on the floor, between his feet, the roll of wire for Tim's aerial.

Tim had been allowed to stay and have dinner with Cherry. He was given a mess tin and a knife, fork and spoon. Cherry called the utensils his 'eating irons.' They'd lined up at a cook tent. Then he tucked into the biggest, most delicious meal he'd had for a long time. The trouble was, he couldn't eat it all.

He thought about the meal now as he adjusted the cat's whisker on the crystal. There was a crackling sound in the earphones. Then a man's voice came through, quite clearly, but Tim couldn't understand a word — he was speaking a foreign language. Tim was about to tune the coil when the voice said:

"And now for our English listeners, a song you all know well."

The man had a heavy accent but Tim understood. There was a pause and the earphones crackled and whistled. Then someone started to sing:

"Tom Pearce, Tom Pearce, lend me your grey mare.
All along, down along, out along lea.
For I want to go to Widdecombe Fair,
With Bill Baxter, John Marshal, Nigel Roland, Pete Fitsimmons ..."

Tim listened, astonished. The man didn't know the song. He got the names wrong, except the first one, and then Uncle Tom Cobley and all.

As soon as the singing stopped there was silence. Tim fiddled with the tuning bead, but it was no use. The station was gone.

At breakfast, Tim told Grandma and Grandpa.

"Maybe it's another version, dear," said Grandma Rose. "Some songs have different words in different places."

"That's a possibility," said Grandpa. "A lot of these old folk songs are like that. Down in the West Country, they'll have a different version than here in Sussex or Kent, or up in the Midlands."

"It wasn't from the West Country or somewhere like that, Grandpa. It was a foreign station," said Tim. "The man said the song was for English listeners."

"Well, that's it, then," said Grandma. "They

don't know the proper words." She stopped talking, her head on one side. "What's that? Oh, no, I've just poured myself a cup of tea."

The sound of the air-raid siren became shrill, rising and falling, and behind it came the now familiar, dreaded throb of a flying-bomb.

In a moment, all were huddled in the Morrison.

"I hate this," said Grandma Rose, angrily. "There's no peace. And I hate to think that we're here and Enid and baby Jane are still at that nursing home. I'm going to suggest she comes home today."

The distant, menacing hum grew to a raucous, deafening racket, shaking the windows, rattling the china on top of the shelter.

"If my new cup gets broken, I'll go over there and wring that man's neck, personally," said Grandpa.

The terrifying noise gradually diminished. There was silence.

"Wait for the all-clear," said Grandpa. "There were six bombs yesterday, remember? And by the way, I meant to tell you — all that talk about gas in these things is so much rubbish."

Chapter 20

Doodlebug Alley

Tim couldn't believe the smell. It was awful! He knelt on the brick floor, feeding more wood to the fire to keep the water boiling for baby Jane's nappies. She seemed to dirty them every five minutes. He closed the cast-iron door to the fire opening and wiped his forehead. It was hot in the scullery. That made the smell worse. He retreated to the kitchen.

"Phew! Shut that door please, Tim." Mum was changing Jane's nappy again. This time it didn't look messy, just wet. Mum snapped the large silver pin in place.

"Who made up that nursery rhyme, Mum?"

"What nursery rhyme, Tim?" Mum picked up baby Jane and laid her in her big, four-wheeled pram. She started to cry.

Tim put his hands over his ears. He'd be glad to be back at school, now that they were home in

Medbury. Except that a flying-bomb had wrecked the big school, and Chalky would be at the convent. Tim sighed. Maybe it wouldn't be so bad. Binky would be there, too.

Mum gently pushed up and down on the handle of the pram, making the springs squeak. The rocking motion seemed to sooth the baby.

"I'll do that, Mummy," said Sarah.

"Thank you, dear." Mum smiled at Tim. "Now, what was this about a nursery rhyme?"

"Nothing really, Mum. It's the one about boys being made of frogs and snails and puppy dogs' tails, and girls being made of sugar and spice and all things nice."

"Well, I've no idea who wrote it, Tim. Why do you want to know?" Mum put the lid on the talcum powder and bundled up the used nappy.

Tim shrugged. "I just think it's daft, that's all. Jane's nappies smell awful!"

Mum laughed. "All babies have smelly nappies, Tim. It doesn't matter if they're girls or boys."

"That's what I mean. The rhyme is daft."

"Well." Mum shrugged. "I suppose you're right. But it just means that boys and girls are different."

"Everybody knows that, Mum. But ... everybody makes smells and things and —"

Mum cut him short. "I don't think we need to go on about it, Tim. It's got nothing to do with smells. The person who made it up might just as easily have said that French people were different from English people because they eat snails and frogs legs, and we eat —"

"They eat snails and frogs?" Sarah stopped rocking the pram. "Grandma said they ate frogs ... but snails? Is that why they don't speak like us?"

Mum burst out laughing and Tim joined in. Usually Mum would get annoyed if he laughed at Sarah's mistakes, but not this time.

"Oh, Sarah." Mum shook her head. "Sometimes you say the funniest things."

"Do I, Mum?" Sarah looked pleased with herself.

Mum kissed Sarah on her forehead and tidied her long fair hair. She sighed and smiled at Tim. "And to think that in just a week, the two of you will be back at school." She gave Sarah a hug.

Tim shrugged. He picked up the damp nappy from the top of the Morrison, and holding it between forefinger and thumb, took it into the scullery. Steam rose from the copper as he removed the wooden lid and dropped the nappy in. It was like a witches' brew boiling in a huge cauldron — slugs and snails, and the tail of a dog, and the horn of a goat ...

Sometimes things were confusing. He replaced the lid. It was time to fetch the newspaper. He wondered if the newsagent had been able to get the *Daily Express* for Mum. Since they'd returned to Medbury, they'd only been able to get the *Daily Mail*. Tim didn't mind, but Sarah was upset. Only the *Daily Express* had the Rupert Bear comic strip.

"Mr. Farnham hasn't been able to get us the *Express* yet, Mum. But look!" Tim pointed excitedly to the map on the front page of the *Daily Mail*. "Look at this map."

Mum looked at the newspaper. She read the words beneath the map. "Allied forces have crossed the Seine south of Rouen and are heading for the rocket coast. That's wonderful," she said. "The sooner we get those flying-bomb launching-sites, the better. Mind you, there's been a lull lately, but we'll still sleep down here in the shelter."

Tim was getting fed up with always sleeping in the Morrison. Baby Jane woke up and cried during the night, and he couldn't listen to his crystal set. He'd thought he'd be able to start sleeping in his room again. He shook his head.

"That's not what I mean, Mum." Tim pointed to the map again. "Look! There!"

Mum looked at the map. "Rouen, you mean?"

"No, Mum. Beneath Rouen, see?"

"Elbeuf?"

"Yes, Mum. Don't you remember?" Tim waited. Mum looked at him and shook her head. "You must remember, Mum. The pigeon! That's where Bill and Sparks came down. And look!" Tim pointed to the paper before Mum could speak. "See that? It says the British and Canadian armies are there. They're piling up guns, tanks and supplies. And then here it says the Canadians are across the river. I wonder if Cherry's there? Maybe he's found Bill?"

"It is wonderful," said Mum. "If Bill's safe, then Grandpa will hear. He'll let us know, somehow."

Tim nodded. It would be wonderful if there was news of Bill. But if only there was news of Dad! There'd been several photographs of Dad at Grandma and Grandpa's, and Tim had thought about him a lot while he was there. But as the weeks and months passed, it got so that Tim only thought of his dad when Mum said a prayer before they lay down in the Morrison. If Mum didn't say that prayer, what then? Tim didn't like to dwell on that.

All morning, Tim kept going back to the newspaper. D-plus 82. It was eighty-two days since the Allied landing in Normandy. An American general, Patton, was only a four-day march from Germany. There was a short report from British Headquarters in France about Hitler losing twenty-five generals since D-Day. But the paper also had an article about a worse weapon than the doodlebug — a very powerful rocket. The newspapers called the doodlebug the V1. This new rocket was the V2, Hitler's second vengeance weapon.

Tim didn't understand. How did Hitler keep getting new things? Why did God let this happen? Sometimes he wondered about praying. Then he thought about Bill. If Bill was at Elbeuf, and if he came back, then maybe ...

The smell of the boiling nappies was back in his nose. He needed some fresh air. "Can I go up to the back field, Mum?"

"But I was about to get lunch, Tim. And you said you'd put the nappies through the mangle for me."

"I know, Mum. But can I do that after we eat?"

"Well, I am behind, and it will give me time to get lunch ready." Mum nodded. "Be back in twenty minutes."

"I will, Mum."

"Can I come, Tim?" Sarah looked at him with that pleading look. "Can I?"

Tim shrugged resignedly. He'd really wanted to be by himself. "Come on, then."

No one else was in the field. Tim nodded. Everyone would be eating. There was the new potato mound, fresh sods laid in a pattern like paving stones, the cracks between the turf brown and moist. It was even longer than the first one, really good for parachuting. He stopped examining the pattern of the thick grass sods, and listened. There was a faint droning, like a swarm of bees. He looked up, searching the sky.

"I can hear something," said Sarah. "Is it a Spitfire?"

Tim strained to listen. The noise was much louder. It was a plane. No, more than one. "I don't know, Sarah. I can't see. The sun's so bright." He shielded his eyes with his hand. "But I think there's more than one."

"There," said Sarah. "I can see one. There it is."

Tim looked where his sister pointed. "Right. And another," he said. "There are two." He watched as the two small planes approached, racing across the sky, gleaming in the sunlight. Then he saw a third, slightly behind the others. The drone of the engines changed from a low, gentle hum to a high-pitched snarl as they rapidly drew nearer. Then, above the roar of the planes, Tim heard the familiar rattle of a flying-bomb. There it was, its tail of flame almost invisible against the brightness of the late summer sky. The fighters were trying to intercept it. The third plane veered, following the course of the doodlebug.

Tim grabbed his sister. "Get down!" he shouted, above the thunder of engines. "Behind the potato mound!"

"We should be home!" Sarah shouted back.

"Down!" shouted Tim. "Down!"

There was the barking, high-pitched crackle of machine gun fire as the planes passed overhead. Thuds came from the other side of the potato mound, heavy, staccato thuds that sent vibrations through the sods, as if giants were kicking at the earthen bank. The sheep in the orchard ran panic-stricken, round and round the square, treed enclosure. Sarah began to cry.

"It's all right, Sarah." Tim put his arm round his sister's shaking shoulders. Then he shouted. "Look! Look!" He jumped up, cheering.

The third plane was flying alongside the doodle-bug, slightly below the level of the deadly bomb. Tim held his breath. He knew what the pilot was doing, knew how dangerous this was. Gradually the plane came up, the tip of the wing ever closer to the black, squat, square-ended wing of the flying-bomb. Sarah held onto Tim's arm, her nails digging into his skin, but he didn't feel anything.

Then the pressure of air between the wings tilted the wing of the pilotless bomb up, the far wing down. The flaming engine roared as if in fury, and the bomb screamed down toward the far hillside.

There was a brilliant yellow and red glow, and the sound of the explosion reached them as a plume of thick, black smoke rose skyward. Tim looked up. The pilot was coming back this way. Why?

"Look, Tim!" Sarah was pointing. Everyone was standing in the road, waving, shouting.

The Spitfire zoomed overhead and then banked, rolling over and over as it sped through the sky. "He's doing the Victory Roll," said Tim.

Then the cheering stopped. In the half-silence, Tim heard a faint whistling noise, as if someone was blowing slowly out between half-closed teeth. It was an eerie, sinister, frightening sound, and Tim felt an icy chill run down his spine. It was a ghost bomb, a floater!

Below the rolling Spitfire was a deadly black cross, gliding purposefully toward them. There was no flame spewing from its tail. Tim had heard of floaters, but he'd never seen one. Sometimes they would glide for only a few seconds before the pointed nose tilted down and the bomb crashed to earth. Sometimes they would glide for minutes, slowly losing height, seeming to choose a target.

The floater lost altitude, but held its course. Tim ducked instinctively as it passed overhead, the deadly whistling tracking its path. It reached the woods at the top of the hill and tilted, slowly. Then, nose down, it dived for the rich, Kent soil. From beyond the trees came the roar of the explosion, and rising to the cloudless sky, the familiar plume of black, sooty smoke and debris.

"That second one came down at Limekiln Farm." Mr. Pearson leaned on the fence, puffing on an old briar pipe.

Tim fed another nappy between the heavy rubber rollers of the mangle on the wash tub. He turned the handle and watched the water ooze out and run noisily into the galvanized iron bucket below. He waited.

"It didn't damage the farm," continued Mr. Pearson, "but it near broke my heart."

Tim stopped turning the handle. He looked at the air raid warden. Mr. Pearson was shaking his head, slowly.

"That old tree had been there ever since I can remember."

"What old tree, Mr. Pearson?"

"The conker tree, Tim. Blown to smithereens, it is!" He chewed on his pipe and glared at the sky. "Been there since my old dad was a boy. Now it's gone. Gone!"

Tim felt anger inside him. There was nothing he could do. The conkers had just begun to ripen, hundreds of them! He turned the handle of the mangle, almost catching his fingers in the rollers as he fed in yet another nappy. This war spoiled everything.

"By the way," said Mr. Pearson. "I don't know whether your Mum has heard since you got back. That man who chased you round the graveyard, the one who came round with the rag and bone cart — he's wanted for murder."

"Murder?" Tim couldn't believe his ears.

Mr. Pearson nodded. He took another puff on his pipe. "He murdered the old man, Ragsy Thatcher. The old chap was probably going to turn him in as a deserter."

"Where did he desert from, Mr. Pearson? The army?"

"No, Tim." The air raid warden shook his head. "He was an aircraftman, on a bomber station north of London. He was caught stealing things from missing pilots and aircrew. Lowest of the low."

PART 3

WIDDECOMBE FAIR

Chapter 21

Coughs and Sneezes ...

"I'll have none of that." The clippie stood at the top of the stairs and pointed at Tim.

"But —"

"No arguing." The conductor looked angry. "I don't like fighting on my bus. You can come downstairs right now!"

"But —" Tim looked for help from the older boys, but they sat there grinning. Chalky had the biggest grin. And Binky hadn't been at school that day, the start of the new term. He had something wrong with his skin. Impetigo, his mother called it. It was so catching, nobody was allowed to go near him.

"Downstairs, this minute!" The clippie pointed to the stairs. "Not another word! I don't want to have to shout with this sore throat." She coughed. "There. Now it's started." She coughed again. "Come on!"

Tim picked up his satchel from the seat and walked slowly down the aisle. It wasn't fair. He hadn't started it. The clippie was coughing as he passed her at the head of the stairs. It was a deep, hacking cough and it did sound bad.

Downstairs, Sarah was sitting on the long seat at the back of the bus. She stared at Tim as he clomped down the last three steps.

"It wasn't my fault," said Tim as he sat down next to his sister. "It was Chalky." He said it loud enough that the conductor would hear.

The clippie smiled. "I'm not daft," she said. "And I'm not deaf." She coughed. "I know it's that big one up there. That's why I told you to come down here."

"But if you knew it was Chalky, why did you get cross with me?" Tim was puzzled, and a little angry.

"Simple." The conductor smiled. "If I told him to come down, he'd take it out on you. This way he thinks he's one up on both of us. He'll leave you alone for a while."

Tim smiled. He hoped the lady conductor was right. Without Binky being around, Chalky could be a problem.

As the bus neared the village green, the crowd upstairs clattered down the metal steps. Before the holidays, before the big school was hit by the doodlebug, they'd have caught the later bus. Chalky was showing off, standing on the edge of the platform, hanging onto the rail. Obviously, his ribs had healed. Before the bus stopped, he jumped off, staggering before regaining his balance.

"Young idiot," said the clippie. "One of these days he'll come a real cropper."

Some of the other children jeered and laughed. Chalky scowled back at them and ran off, across the green.

Tim and Sarah hung back from the crowd as the bus sped down the road. Brown and yellow leaves scurried after it, tumbling over and over as if chasing the rear wheels.

"Can you see Chalky?" asked Sarah.

Tim shook his head. He peered down the road as they passed the newsagent's. "I hope the conductor's right and he'll leave us alone." He took Sarah's hand. "Come on."

They walked slowly. A short way ahead were some older men, at the entrance to Limekiln Farm. They were still clearing the debris of the conker tree, branches white as bleached bones, huge splinters of wood like giant teeth biting the soil in agony. Tim still hated thinking about the tree. He let go of Sarah's hand and stopped to watch the men. He looked beyond the busy workmen. Chalky had reached the top of the hill. He didn't look back. Good. They walked on, passing the entrance to the farm.

"Let's have a look at the crater," said Tim.

"Mummy will be waiting." Sarah looked doubtful.

"Just two minutes. Don't let anyone see you." Tim scrambled up the bank and through the hedge. "Come on." Even though the hedge was still standing, it was leafless. The blast from the bomb had stripped it bare.

Sarah followed, pulling her satchel behind her. It caught in the tangled branches. "I'm stuck," she called.

"Sh!" Tim placed his finger to his lips. "Not so loud." He freed the satchel and turned back, picking his way through the branches and slivers crunching and cracking underfoot. He knew the crater had been searched carefully by the army, the Home Guard, the A.R.P. and everyone else official. Then the locals had combed through it too. Before he got impetigo, Binky had shown Tim some shrapnel that he said came from the nose of the doodlebug. Tim hadn't been allowed to visit the crater, and this was the first time he'd been on his own — well, with Sarah.

His eyes scanned the ground as he approached the circle of fresh-banked earth at the edge of the hole. It was hard-packed from the many feet before him. The sour, acrid smell of burning still rose from the scorched earth. He climbed the bank and peered down into the crater. Large chunks of blackened, twisted steel lay half-buried in the soil. But it was obvious that anything that could be carried, or hidden in a pocket, was gone. Sarah struggled up beside him.

"It smells awful." She screwed up her nose. "I want to go home."

"All right." Tim kicked dejectedly at the earth. Sarah was right. There was no point staying here. He kicked again, angrily, and his toe dislodged something small. It went tumbling, rolling down the slope. It was probably a stone. But was it? Tim's heart quickened. It didn't look like the usual flint or chalk. He watched as it came to rest. It wasn't a stone. He half ran, half jumped down the slope, spreading his arms to keep his balance. He bent and picked up the small but heavy metal object. It was a little bigger than the bullets he'd dug out of the potato mound.

"Oy! Out of there, young'un!"

Tim thrust the thing into his pocket and scrambled back up the side of the crater. Had the man seen?

"Off you go, both of you! You could get hurt down there." The workman stood on the other side. "Off you go!"

"I said we should have gone home," said Sarah.

Tim was too excited to answer back. "Come on!" He headed for the hedge. As he pushed through the branches, his eyes were attracted by something nestling in the thick, dry grass around the roots of the hawthorn. It was a conker, the shiny, brown surface dulled and scratched.

"We'll plant it," said Mr. Pearson. "Once they've done clearing, I'll go and see old Arthur at the farm, and we'll plant it. We'll grow another tree. We'll not let them stop us Kentish men playing conkers! Will we?"

Tim shook his head. But it would be ages before the tree grew and before it had conkers of its own!

"What's that other thing you have there?"

Tim stared at his hand. He hadn't realized he'd taken out his find from the bomb crater. Mr. Pearson was a warden. He'd take it away. Reluctantly, Tim held it out.

"Hm." Mr. Pearson took the piece of metal. He rubbed away some of the mud and turned it over and over. "Hm. Looks like an old spark plug to me. Not much good now." He handed it back. "Time for my supper." He smiled. "Keep that conker safe, Tim."

Tim waved hurriedly, and rushed down the path. A spark plug! Could it be? It had to be one of those special plugs for launching the flying-bombs. No one had one of those. By the coal-bin he rubbed off the remaining mud. There it was, the name — BOSCH! He'd put it with the bullets from the Spitfire. Binky would be really envious.

When Tim got off the school bus the next afternoon, he was shivering with cold. And he felt sick. Every day for the past week, Sister had made him sit at his desk and drink his milk while she watched. He'd thought that with a new teacher he might have been able to get away with not drinking the dreaded liquid, but obviously she'd been told. His mouth still tasted funny and his tongue was thick and fuzzy. Plain milk was awful!

Chalky shambled on ahead. He'd been very quiet on the bus, not bothering anyone. He stopped and leaned against a tree, his hand to his head. Sarah was down the road with the older girls. Tim waited. What was Chalky up to? Then he saw the older boy's shoulders heave and Chalky doubled over, clutching at the tree, retching. He was being sick! Tim felt his own stomach heave. The acid smell of vomit reached his nose. He doubled over, heaving, feeling as if his insides were about to be torn out.

"Argh ... argh." Chalky was still being sick. "I feel awful."

"I'm sure it's the milk, Mum," said Tim, later.

"I'll have to speak to Sister." Mum shook her head. "There's no point in you being sick like this over a bottle of milk."

The next day, Tim refused to drink his milk. Sister looked sternly at him and then reached out. Tim shrank back.

"I'm not going to hurt you, Athelstan. Let me feel your forehead." The nun's fingers felt cool and soothing. Tim shut his eyes.

"Hm. You're running a temperature. Come with me. You can lie down in the sick bay for a while."

"Chalky was in there too, Mum," said Tim, as he lay in bed that evening.

"Well, you get some rest, Tim. I expect you've caught a chill." Mum felt his forehead. "Not enough decent food to keep you children healthy." She shook her head. "How much longer can this wretched war drag on? It's wicked."

The next day, Tim had a painfully sore throat and his head throbbed, a pounding ache that seemed to stretch down from his scalp, deep into his brain, to the back of his eyes. He hardly knew where he was. He tried listening to the crystal set, but his fingers were too shaky to tune it properly. He did think he'd heard someone singing "Widdecombe Fair," but he couldn't be sure. Sometimes he wasn't sure if he really had tried to listen.

Two days later, a rash appeared — small, bright red spots, closely set, like a sunburn with goose pimples.

Through a haze, Tim heard the doctor. "He'll have to be isolated, Mrs. Athelstan. Scarlet fever is very contagious. I've just come from the White's house. Their boy has it too. I'll get the ambulance for both of them."

"Don't hit me, Dad! Please, don't get angry!"

Tim struggled awake. What was happening?

Two white-smocked nurses stood on either side of the other bed in the room. Tim knew that one of them was called Mrs. Tait. She always seemed to be there when he woke up. He didn't know the second one.

"Hold still, lad," said Mrs. Tait, gently.

Chalky tossed and turned in his bed, moaning.

"Poor lad," said the other nurse. "He's delirious with the fever." She wiped Chalky's forehead with a cloth. "What's this about his dad hitting him? Do you know?"

"Yes." Mrs Tait nodded. "He was muttering that when he was first brought in. I asked his mum about it next day, when she was visiting. She said Mr. White wasn't let into the services, not even the A.R.P. or the Home Guard. He has these asthma attacks, she said. He doesn't like it one bit, being stuck at home while everyone else is off fighting the Hun, and he's taken out his frustrations on the boy."

"Stupid man," said the other nurse. "I can understand him being frustrated, but the boy will turn into a bully if he keeps that up."

Mrs. Tait nodded. "His mum told me poor Brian's been taunted by some of the children in their neighbourhood. They call him a coward, say he's like his dad that way." She shook her head. "No wonder he fights."

"Children can be cruel sometimes."

"There, there, lad," said Mrs. Tait as Chalky

started moaning. She rinsed a cloth in an enamel bowl and squeezed out the water.

Tim listened to the water dribbling into the bowl. He wished it was dribbling down his throat, it hurt so badly.

"That one," said Mrs. Tait, "young Tim, keeps calling out 'L-for-Lucky Lancaster,' and something about a gas mask, and not being scared anymore."

"Must have had a fright, poor lad."

"Probably. But we'll have to watch these two. Dr. Hogg told me they had a fight before the summer. That one broke this one's ribs."

"That one? I can't believe it. He's much smaller."

"Well, that's what the doctor said."

Tim floated back into the quiet of his head, away from the raging pain in his throat.

Chapter 22

... Spread Diseases

Tim stood on the cabinet beside his bed. His throat was a lot better. The thick, white medicine he'd been given tasted awful, like liquid chalk. It stuck to the roof of his mouth, and when he ran his tongue along the back of his teeth, they felt rough, like fine sandpaper. It was worse than school milk, but at least it seemed to be doing him some good.

He looked down at Chalky. Chalky had been really sick. The doctor had come several times a day during the first week. Now he came once a day.

Chalky's eyes were closed. He breathed noisily through his mouth. Tim tried not to do that. If he slept with his mouth open, it made his throat dry. Then it started to ache all over again.

He shrugged. It was good to be feeling better. The rash was gone, but his skin had turned scaly and was starting to flake and peel.

He peered out of the window. It was a stupid place to put a window, up so high that you couldn't see out without standing on something. The isolation hospital was built in an L shape. Tim's room was in the short section of the L, on the ground floor. The window faced the rear. Across a brick-paved yard was another building. Smoke belched out of a tall, round, red chimney stack. The top of the stack was black and sooty. To the right of the stack was a small wooded area. A squirrel was busy collecting cob nuts and burying them, its red tail flicking this way and that as it looked round, as if making sure that no one saw where each morsel was hidden.

Tim watched for a while. It was good to see a red squirrel. Dad said they were the true British breed, not the grey ones from America. The squirrel bounded over to a tree, streaked up the trunk and scurried into the branches. What had disturbed it? A magpie flew down from the roof. It scratched at the ground, then picked up something in its beak and ate it. It hopped to another spot and scratched again. It was cracking open a cob nut! Tim couldn't believe it. The magpie had watched the squirrel burying food for the winter, and now the bird was stealing it. Tim was about to bang on the window to frighten the bird away when he felt a hand on the back of his leg.

"Mind you don't fall." The voice was quiet, but firm. "Now, I want you off there and back between those sheets."

Tim looked down at Nurse Tait. She was really quite nice, but strict. Her eyes were a deep blue. Her dark brown hair was pulled back tightly, beneath the starched white hat, into a bun at the back.

She held out her free hand. "Hold on while I help you down."

Tim jumped, landing in the middle of the mattress.

"Now, I don't want to see you up there again. Is that clear?"

"Yes, Mrs. Tait."

The nurse busied herself tidying the sheets.

"I finished those books," said Tim. "Now I don't have anything to read."

The nurse nodded. "Well, at least one of you is getting better." She looked over at Chalky. "I think he's over the worst, though. Another day should see him right. Both of you were really sick."

"Will I have to stay in this room with him all the time?" asked Tim

Mrs. Tait looked at him. Her eyes seemed to search his mind. "I hear that you have had fights." She shook her head. "No fighting in here, or you'll have me to deal with."

"I don't want to fight," said Tim. "It's Chalky that starts it."

"Is it?" The nurse stared at him. "I thought you were the one who broke his ribs."

"Only because he was hurting my sister. He always picks on people smaller than he is. Anyway, I didn't mean to break his ribs." Tim looked at the nurse. "Is it true that his dad hits him?"

"Where did you hear that?"

"I heard you talking about it the other night."

Mrs. Tait nodded. "I see. Well, it's true, Tim. Mrs. White told me. That's probably why he acts the way he does. He gets bullied at home, so he does the same to others. But don't go talking about it."

"I won't, Nurse Tait." Tim looked across to the bed where Chalky lay, snoring.

"Now, stay in bed and I'll fetch you something to read, though what it will be I really don't know." She paused. "I don't suppose you'd like the paper, would you?"

"Do you have the *Daily Express*?" asked Tim.

The nurse laughed. "Picky about what you read? I'll see what I can do."

"So, what's the news?" The nurse smiled as she brought in a steaming enamel mug of tea.

Tim turned back to the front page. "It's not as interesting as sometimes. They say the war will go on right through winter. See." Tim pointed to the headline: BLACK-OUT WINTER.

"And look at this!" Tim went on. "Hitler's making boys of sixteen go in the army!"

"No!" The nurse looked to where Tim pointed at the report in the late news section. "That's terrible!"

"Well, at least they get to do something," said Tim. "I can never do anything."

"Don't be silly, Tim." Nurse Tait had that strict look again. "What a ridiculous thing to say!"

Tim felt uncomfortable. He didn't know why he'd blurted that out. Maybe it was because he was feeling useless again, sick here in the isolation hospital. He wasn't even home to look after Mum and Sarah.

"Sending children to war is a despicable, evil thing," said the nurse. "That man will surely go to hell."

Tim nodded. "Mr. Churchill says Hitler's a war criminal." He took a sip of tea. It travelled down slowly, over his tonsils. It felt good. It didn't hurt anymore. "Have you heard that new song?"

Nurse Tait smiled. "There are so many new songs, Tim. Is it that new one Bing Crosby sings?"

Tim shook his head. "It's not that kind of song. It's one about Hitler and Mr. Churchill."

"Well, come on. Don't keep me in suspense."

Tim took another sip of tea. He wasn't sure he could sing, even though his throat wasn't so bad anymore. He swallowed.

"When the war is over, Hitler will be dead.
He hopes to go to heaven with a crown upon his head.
But the Lord will say, 'No! I'm sending you below,
There's only room for Churchill here, so cheery-eery-oh!'"

Nurse Tait chuckled. "Not as bad as some I hear." She sighed. "I just wish this war was really over."

Tim thought she looked tired, like Mum. No wonder. He could remember seeing only Nurse Tait and the other nurse, the whole time he'd been here, even at night.

"Do you live at the hospital?" he asked.

Nurse Tait laughed. "No, Tim, I don't. I live a short way down the road, this side of Tonbridge."

"Tonbridge?" Tim looked down at the newspaper. "Here it says they're going to send hundreds of Italian prisoners of war to a large farm near Tonbridge."

"You must be joking. Let me have a look." Nurse Tait reached for the paper. "Does it say which farm?"

Tim shook his head. "I'm not joking. But it doesn't say which farm, just a big one."

"Hm. I wonder?"

"My dad went missing in Italy," said Tim, quietly. "But maybe he got to Switzerland. See!" He pointed to a small report on the front page. "Six hundred escaped British prisoners left Switzerland yesterday, to come home. It says a lot come from London. We used to live in London."

The nurse nodded slowly. "I saw that," she said. "My brother is missing too. He was taken prisoner in France, in nineteen-forty. Then he escaped." She closed her eyes, putting her hand to her forehead. "We haven't had any word since." She shook her head. "Four years!"

"We haven't heard from Dad, either," said Tim. "We hoped we'd hear from the Red Cross." He shook his head. "Dad's cousin from Canada is missing too. He's a bomber pilot. He was shot down over France."

"Oh, dear." Mrs. Tait shook her head.

"He bailed out," said Tim. "We know where he is."

"How? How do you know that?"

Tim explained about Sparks and Wing Commander Sparklet.

"Isn't that wonderful! Maybe they'll join up with the Canadian army." The nurse took the newspaper. "Now, where did I see that? Ah, here it is — Dunkirk. The Canadians have agreed with the French Red Cross to let civilians out of Dunkirk. It says here that children and sick and old people are streaming out. But they've only got until six o'clock tonight, then the fighting starts again. Terrible."

Tim nodded. He'd read that. Maybe Bill would meet the Canadian army. Maybe ... He shook his head. Suddenly he felt tired. Thinking about Dad and Bill ... not knowing ... It was the not knowing all the time that was the worst.

The nurse took the mug from his hand. "Have a nap." She looked at Chalky. "I'll be back in an hour with hot soup and fresh bread from the hospital bakery."

"So, this is where ye've got to, young Tim."

Tim sniffed. There was a strong smell of coal and smoke in the room. He opened his eyes, and then rubbed them. Something was strange. He knew it was the beekeeper, Mr. Runciman, but ...

"This is my wee, young brother. Sometimes folk think we're twins." Mr. Runciman smiled at the grey-bearded figure standing beside him. "He works here."

The second Mr. Runciman smiled but said nothing.

Tim stopped rubbing his eyes. He wasn't seeing double. He looked from one to the other. The two men were almost identical, but the younger one wore a boiler suit, and his hands were ingrained with black dust and soot. He didn't look very young, though, and he wasn't small.

"I went to see thy mother, when I heard," said the beekeeper. "She sends her love." He nodded. "I often visit wee Alec here, so I said I'd pop in and see ye." He reached into an old cloth bag. "I've brought ye some honey. It's good for the throat. A natural antiseptic."

"Thanks, Mr. Runciman." Tim could almost taste the honey. Maybe, if it was an antiseptic, he wouldn't have to take so much of the thick, white, milky medicine. "Mum can't come and visit me."

The old man nodded. "I know. Scarlet fever is very catching for wee bairns like Sarah and Jane. 'Coughs and sneezes spread diseases,' my old mother used to say. But it doesn't hit old codgers like Alec and myself."

Tim nodded. "I'm glad Sarah and baby Jane didn't get it. But I've got to stay here for another two weeks, so has Chalky."

Mr. Runciman glanced at the other bed. "Ah, yes. Where is that young bully?"

"He's getting a bath, for his skin. It's peeling. Mine's still peeling, too." Tim looked at the beekeeper. "I feel sorry for him."

Mr. Runciman raised his eyebrows. "Feel sorry for him now? Is that so?"

Tim nodded. "He bullies people because he thinks they laugh at him."

"Does he now? And why is that?"

"Because of his dad," said Tim. "His dad can't get in the army or the Home Guard." He told the two men about Mr. White. Then he remembered. Nurse Tait had said not to talk about it.

"Mm. Maybe this Chalky needs a friend," said the beekeeper. "What do ye think, Alec?"

"Mm. Maybe so."

Tim waited, but Mr. Runciman's brother said no more.

"Maybe," said the beekeeper, "ye could show Tim and young Chalky round the place." He looked at his brother. "Maybe ye could show them the secret passage?"

Secret passage! Tim waited. Young, grey-haired Mr. Runciman nodded slowly. "Aye, maybe I could do that. Maybe."

Chapter 23

A Morale Booster

"I don't want to go down any stupid old secret passage." Chalky White stared angrily at Tim. "Why do you keep on bothering me? Why can't you shut up?"

Tim was getting angry himself. He was trying to be nice, but every time he did, Chalky got upset.

"Who wants to go down a stupid old tunnel, anyway?" Chalky plumped himself down on his bed. "It's not a real secret passage, just a tunnel."

"It's something to do," said Tim. "You haven't been down there yet."

Chalky glared at him. "Well I don't want to go with you. I can go by myself if I want to. I'm not scared."

"I didn't say you were scared." Tim glared back. "You're always thinking people think you're scared."

Chalky's eyes narrowed. His fists were clenched, the knuckles white. He turned away, rolling onto his side, facing the wall.

Tim shrugged. He'd tried. It had been fun helping the young Mr. Runciman shovel coal into the gaping mouths of the furnaces. The beekeeper's brother had collected him after the midday meal and shown him the damp, narrow dark tunnel that connected the main building to his 'lair,' as he called it. The smell of coal and smoke had stayed on Tim's pyjamas throughout the evening, reminding him of the warmth of the boiler room and the little room where Mr. Runciman had his tea, and honey sandwiches.

The entrance to the tunnel was off the main hall, behind the straight-backed wooden benches where visitors had to wait. The door looked like one of the old, dark oak panels that covered the walls, stretching up from the black-and-white tiled floor to the arched, black-beamed ceiling.

No one seemed to speak out loud in the hall. Everyone whispered, as if they were in church.

Mr. Runciman had whispered, "It's down here."

Now, standing in the corridor once more, Tim couldn't see the door. He felt along the panelled wall, his fingers searching for the hole in the wood. There it was, and there was the catch. The door swung open. Cold, damp air flowed out into the corridor. Tim shivered. He felt as if someone was watching him. He looked back. There was no one in the hall. As he stepped onto the top step, the door closed behind him.

He stood on the top step, waiting for his eyes to become accustomed to the gloom. Then he made his way down the old stone stairway, his right hand on the cold wall. It was damp and slimy near the bottom. Somewhere water dripped. It echoed down the tunnel. In the distance was a faint, yellow glow. He set off, feeling his way along the wall. Gradually the tunnel became warmer.

At the end of the passage was a small, windowless, stone-walled room. Tim thought he heard a cough behind him. He peered back, but the light from the room had blinded his eyes to the darkness of the tunnel. He heard another cough. He smiled. It wasn't coming from the tunnel. It came from beyond the door on the other side of the room.

He crossed the floor, skirting round the table laid with cups and plates, and bread and honey. He looked back, still smiling. Good old young Mr. Runciman. Chalky was stupid. Tim pushed the door open and stepped into the boiler room. The mountain of glistening black coal loomed high.

"Just keep yer trap shut, old man!"

Tim stopped in his tracks. That wasn't young Mr. Runciman's voice, but it *was* vaguely familiar.

"This 'ere knife's as sharp as a razor." The

speaker coughed. "Bloomin' smoke! Get's in me throat."

Now Tim recognized the voice. It was Sciver! He was sure it was. Sciver the murderer, Sciver the thief from Bill's station. He crept forward, stepping carefully over the pieces of coal littering the floor. There must have been a delivery down the wide-mouthed brick chute, and Mr. Runciman hadn't had time to clear up.

"Never expected to see me, did yer, old man?"

Tim shivered as the man laughed. It was a cold, dry, throaty sound, out of place in the warm cosiness of the boiler room.

Tim peered round the front of the boiler. Mr. Runciman lay huddled partly on the ground, partly on the pile of coal. Sciver stood over him, waving a large knife slowly this way and that.

"Old Ragsy didn't expect to see me, either." Sciver prodded Mr. Runciman with the toe of a muddy boot. "He was goin' to tell." He narrowed his eyes, and gave Mr. Runciman a warning look. "Well, 'e won't tell no one, now."

Mr. Runciman raised himself on one elbow. He shook his head slowly from side to side. Tim could see an angry red welt on his forehead. Sciver placed a boot roughly on the old man's chest and pushed. With a grunt, Mr. Runciman fell back. His half-closed eyes widened as he saw Tim.

"Now I want yer 'elp, old man." The knife flashed in the light from the solitary bulb hanging in the centre of the ceiling. "I need a place to rest for a day or two, maybe down 'ere? It's nice and warm down 'ere." Sciver looked round and Tim barely had time to duck back behind the furnace.

"There must be somewhere."

Tim heard footsteps coming his way. He ran on tiptoe, back behind the furnace.

"What's be'ind this furnace? What's that light?"

"Nothing, Sid," said Mr. Runciman.

"Don't lie to me, you stupid old man! Or else."

"Or else what, Sid?"

"You know."

"Ha!" The boilerman laughed. "Killing old men. Ye are a coward, Sid, as ye were when ye were younger."

"Shut up!"

"Always the bully, Sid. Always picking on those that can't fight back. Coward!"

"Why, you — I'll —"

Tim heard a rumbling, faint at first, then steadily growing louder. It couldn't be another delivery of coal. He peered round the back of the boiler. The old man was scrambling up the shiny black mound, sending coal cascading to the concrete floor below. What was he doing? Trying to get to the only way out, the chute? Mr. Runciman saw Tim. He half-waved, shaking his head.

Sciver was standing below the old man. He raised the knife. He was going to throw it!

Tim yelled, "Mr. Runciman!" He started to scramble up the side of the coal pile toward the old man.

"What the —" Sciver whirled round. "Why you —" He aimed the knife at Tim. His eyes narrowed. "I've seen you before, you little —"

"Don't do it, Sid. Run, Tim!"

"Shut up!" shouted Sciver. "Shut up!"

Tim couldn't move. The eyes of the murderer seemed to hold him, staring, unblinking. He shivered.

"You stay where you are, you little beggar! Down 'ere, old man. Be sharp about it."

Mr. Runciman hesitated, then slid down the side of the mound of coal, gathering speed as he neared the bottom. Sciver moved quickly to one side. He seemed to know what the boilerman was about to do. With a shout, Mr. Runciman launched himself into the air, but Sciver was ready. He kicked out, his boot hitting the old man on the side of the head. With a moan, Mr. Runciman fell to the floor in a crumpled heap. Sciver crouched down, balancing the knife in his hand. Without taking his eyes off Mr. Runciman, he called to Tim, "Down 'ere, you. Come on!" He held the knife to Mr. Runciman's throat. "Now!"

Tim slithered to the front of the mound and slid slowly down. Sciver grabbed him roughly by the hair and peered into his face.

"I know you. You were at the church. 'It me

with a snowball. 'Ow'd you get 'ere?" He yanked Tim's hair. The pain was terrible, but Tim wasn't going to show it.

"Leave the boy alone, Sid." Mr. Runciman looked up from the floor. One eye was closed, the skin above and below torn, red and swollen. "I'll do what ye want."

"Shut up!" Sciver motioned with the knife. "I'm not talking to you." He put his face close to Tim's, his mouth a pale, grim line outlined by dark stubble.

Tim had had time to think. He wasn't going to tell about the tunnel if he could help it. He yelled as the man yanked on his hair. He let tears roll down his cheeks.

"Ha. That's more like it." Sciver looked him up and down. "Now, tell me what's behind the furnace."

"Just a room," said Mr. Runciman. "It's where I have my meals."

"That's right," said Tim. "I was having a honey sandwich and some tea when I heard you."

"Perfect." Sciver nodded. "The boy can stay with me while you get me some clothes, food and other things I need." He leered at Tim. "You'll like that, won't you?"

Tim shuddered. This man was ... what was it Bill had said? A swine. That was it.

"Are ye not scared I'll turn ye in, Sid Thatcher?"

Sciver's fingers tightened in Tim's hair, his eyes narrowed. "If yer so much as breathe a word, or bring anyone back with yer, the boy gets it. It won't matter to me. I'll swing anyway if I'm taken, for murderin' old Ragsy."

Tim shuddered. He remembered what Mrs. Pearson had said about Sciver's eyes — "Like a sexton measuring you for a grave, or an undertaker for a coffin." Suddenly, the boiler room felt as icy cold as the snow-covered cemetery when he'd first seen Sciver. He had to escape. Sciver must be caught.

"But they'll miss the boy," said Mr. Runciman. "They'll start a search for him."

"Not 'ere they won't. Not if yer says 'e ain't been 'ere."

"All right." Mr. Runciman propped himself up on one elbow. "But don't ye harm the boy. I don't care what ye do to me, but leave him be, do ye hear? What do ye want me to get?"

"I'll tell yer when I've 'ad some food." Sciver let go of Tim's hair. "Lead the way. Get up, old man."

Tim knew his only chance was to run for the tunnel. But if he did, Sciver would kill Mr. Runciman, and then come after him. It was no good shouting for help now or in the tunnel. No one would hear a thing.

"Move!" Sciver gave him a shove in the back.

Tim couldn't remember clearly what happened next. He remembered pretending to fall, picking up a lump of coal and throwing it at the murderer.

Sciver screamed with rage as the coal hit him in the eye. He let go of Mr. Runciman and lunged forward to grab Tim. Then a figure shot out from the shadows behind the boiler. It was Chalky, a long coal shovel held straight out in front of him, like a lance. Sciver was taken by surprise as the broad metal scoop of the shovel hit him in the stomach.

"Ugh!" Sciver bent double and dropped his knife. "Ugh!" He dropped to his knees as Mr. Runciman hit him, with both hands clenched, on the back of his neck. "Ugh! Ugh!" He covered his face as Tim rained lumps of coal at him. Then, he collapsed on the floor as Chalky hit him again with the shovel, the metal ringing as it bounced off his head.

Chapter 24

Stir Up, Stir Up!

"If Chalky hadn't hit him with the shovel, Grandpa, I don't know what I'd have done."

"Mr. Runciman would have done something, Tim. Anyway, you hit him square in the eye with that first lump of coal. That would hurt, and grit would have got in, too. And I'll bet you would've hit him again." Grandpa smiled. He looked across the kitchen. "Mm. That smells good."

They'd all come home from the old church by the village green. Tim knew that the prayer for this last Sunday before the Christmas season — "Stir up, we beseech Thee," and the bit about "the fruit" — didn't really have anything to do with stirring cake and pudding mixture, even though he'd once thought it did.

But everyone called this Stir Up Sunday, because it was the day when special puddings and cakes were made in readiness for Christmas Day, only a few short weeks away. And the words of the prayer did, sort of, talk about it, didn't they?

Tim had been home for three weeks. He'd only returned to school on Wednesday, after a final visit from the doctor. He'd missed a lot of school, but he'd enjoyed being home. While he rested in bed, he listened to the crystal set. The fighting in France and Holland continued. Mr. Churchill said that the greatest fighting was yet to come. This worried Tim. Mr. Churchill said it was at the end of the struggle that wars were won or lost. The next day he talked about the V2, Hitler's silent vengeance rocket. It flew so high, and so fast — faster than the speed of sound — that you couldn't hear it, like you could a doodlebug. Hitler always came up with something.

But there was good news. A reporter said there would be nuts for Christmas this year — almonds, filberts and peanuts. Mum had got hers, and she'd managed to get some dried fruit. And the big battleship, the *Tirpitz*, the pride of Hitler's navy, had been sunk by twenty-nine Lancaster bombers. Wouldn't Bill have liked to be part of that?

Mrs. White and Chalky had come for tea, twice. The first time wasn't bad, except when Chalky's mother made him apologize again, for dragging Sarah off to see the "three-legged man." Chalky's face went bright red. Tim hadn't been asked to apologize for breaking Chalky's ribs. He'd thought about it but decided to keep quiet.

The second visit was two Sundays ago. Binky was over impetigo and came by to hear the story of the capture of Sciver. Mum and Mrs. White chatted happily, but the atmosphere between Chalky and Binky was tense. Tim wanted all of them to be friends. He'd got on well with Chalky for the last two weeks at hospital, and he would never forget Chalky's courage in helping tackle Sciver. He could have left him and Mr. Runciman with the murderer, and gone back to the main building to raise the alarm. But Tim realised that Chalky would never be quite the friend that Binky was. He was startled out of his thoughts by Grandma Rose.

"Stir up! Stir up time!" Grandma carried the bowl of pudding mixture to the Morrison and waved a large wooden spoon in the air. "Now, is everyone ready to sing?"

There was a chorus of "yes," "aye" and "of course" in reply. Grandpa always said "aye" at stir up time. No one knew why, not even Grandpa.

"Who's going to stir the pudding first?"

"Me, Grandma!" Sarah jumped up. She knocked over her chair in her excitement.

Above the clatter of the falling chair, a voice boomed out. "How about me?" The back door was half open and an icy blast of winter air whistled into the kitchen.

"What? Shut that —" Mum stared at the door.

"Bill!" shouted Tim.

"Bill!" screamed Sarah.

"Well, give me the spoon." Bill leaned on a sturdy brier walking stick and lowered his kit-bag to the floor. He slammed the door behind him with his free hand. "Gee, it's cold out there."

"Glory be!" said Grandma Rose, breaking the silence. "Glory be!"

"Well, well, my boy." Grandpa crossed the kitchen and hugged Bill. "Wonderful to see you."

"It is, Bill ... wonderful." Mum smiled. But Tim could tell, from the tone of her voice and the set of her mouth, that she was struggling not to cry. She took the spoon from Grandma Rose. "Here, Bill. Come and stir up. And sing everyone! *Dear old Christmas pudding,*" she began.

"*Dear old Christmas pudding comes to see us once again.*" Bill's voice filled the kitchen.

"Good heavens," said Grandpa. "Do you know the words, Bill?"

"Of course, Uncle George. It's a tradition. Mum always sings the 'Christmas Pudding Song' on Stir Up Sunday, and on Christmas Day when she brings in the pudding."

"Of course" Grandpa nodded. "You know, that song must be at least a hundred years old. Dear old Mum used to sing it, and she'd learned it from her mother."

"Well, don't let age hold us up," said Grandma. "Sing, everybody!"

The sound echoed through old Bramley Cottage:

"Dear old Christmas Pudding comes to see us once again.
Let's all join in the chorus and sing this glad refrain.
There are many famous puddings,
And they are both great and small,
But dear old Christmas Pudding is the monarch of them all.
So sing 'Tra La La La' to the monarch of the table,
With its currants, nuts and spice,
And all things that are nice.
Come, sing 'Tra La La La' as loud as you are able.
And the one who sings the loudest,
Will have the biggest slice."

The pots rattled as the kitchen was filled with singing and shouts and laughter. Then Bill dug the spoon into the mixture and stirred it round and round.

"Don't forget to wish," said Grandma.

"Believe me, I won't," said Bill. Now ..." He paused. "Wait a minute." He limped over to his kit-bag and reached inside. "Aha!" He held up a bottle. "French brandy. Mum always likes a drop of brandy in the mixture."

"That's the ticket," said Grandpa. "Just what we needed."

Bill hobbled back over to the Morrison,

uncorked the bottle and poured a liberal amount of the pungent-smelling amber liquid into the bowl. He gave the mixture a quick stir. "Who's next?"

"Sarah," said Grandpa George. "Then Tim." He reached into his pocket and held up a small, sparkling silver coin. "And don't let's forget this." He dropped the threepenny piece into the mixture. "Stir up!"

Tim waited. Sarah stirred and stirred. What was she doing? "I made a really big wish," she said. "I —"

"Don't tell anyone," shouted Tim, "or it won't come true!" He knew what he'd wish for. The singing, the smell of the kitchen, the silver threepenny piece, and Bill with his fair, bristly moustache, had brought visions of Dad to his mind. He hadn't remembered Dad like this for ages — Dad smiling, the two of them tobogganing on Hampstead Heath, singing "Good King Wenceslas" on the way back. For the longest time, he'd thought that a good king named Wensas had last looked out. But what he liked best was thinking of himself as the page, trudging along behind, treading in his dad's footsteps. Where was Dad? He was shaken out of his thoughts again.

"I've finished!" shouted Sarah. "Stir up!"

"We were coned by searchlights," said Bill. "Only this time I couldn't get out of them. It seemed as if they were glued to us. The flak was awful, ripping chunks of metal out of the old lady." He shook his head. "We didn't have a chance. Lucky we all got out alive."

"What happened to your leg?" asked Tim. "Did it get hit by bullets?"

Bill shook his head. "It was stupid. Not a scratch after all that fire, and then I miss the field I'm aiming for and land in a tree on the edge of a large wood."

"In a tree?" Sarah started to giggle.

"It's not funny, Sarah." Tim glared across the table.

"Well, it is, in a way," said Bill. "There I am, in this tree, hanging from a branch so high I could barely see the ground. That bit was funny. But I had to get down before the enemy patrols found me." He nodded and breathed in deeply. "I was scared, believe me. I'd heard of guys being shot up as they hung helplessly in their harnesses like that."

"Terrible!" said Grandma. "What did you do, Bill?"

"Well, I didn't have a knife, Aunt Rose. I couldn't cut myself down. Anyway, I was a bit high up for that. And I couldn't shout to the others. That would bring the patrols running if they were near."

"So what did you do, Bill?" asked Tim.

Bill smiled. "I started to swing, kicking out like I used to on the swings in the local park at St. Catharines, back and forth, back and forth. I got up quite a speed, getting closer and closer to the branch I was aiming for. The branch I was snagged on was beginning to bounce, and it was creaking so loudly I was sure the patrols would get me. My heart was hammering nineteen to the dozen, I can tell you." He looked round the table.

Tim waited. What had happened?

"Well, the branch broke," said Bill. "I came tumbling down, hitting the lower branches. How the 'chute didn't get snagged again, I'll never know. But I hit the ground awkwardly, and my leg buckled beneath me. There was a loud crack, almost as loud as a rifle shot."

"Oh, the pain," said Grandma, putting her hand to her mouth. "It must have been agony."

Bill nodded. "It was painful, Aunt Rose. I couldn't move, and I lay there, not caring if the patrols did find me. But two of the guys had seen it all from the field. They had my 'chute off and buried in no time flat. Then they carried me across the field."

"Why didn't you hide in the wood?" Tim was puzzled.

"That's the first place anyone would look, Tim," said Grandpa.

Bill nodded. "That's right. Then we heard a truck racing up the road. We hid in a ditch. There were twenty men with rifles. They fanned out across the field, following the route we'd taken, but in the opposite direction. They found the buried parachute pretty quickly. That was a stroke of luck really, because they headed into the wood, probably thinking we'd taken cover there. They were in the wood a long time. My leg was killing me." Bill shut his eyes and sighed. "Fortunately they didn't know one of us was injured. They left. Obviously they thought we'd escaped before they arrived." He smiled. "The rest you know."

Tim nodded. Bill hadn't known that Sparks had seen all the parachutes open and reported everyone safe. Two days later, Bill had been taken to the farm outside Elbeuf by the French Resistance. Sparks and the others were there. It was the farmer who'd set his broken leg. And, as Nurse Tait had said, Bill did meet up with the Canadian troops, but he hadn't seen Cherry. He'd met his friend's sergeant only to learn that Cherry had died the day after the Lincoln and Welland Regiment landed in France.

Tim lay in bed, warming his feet on the old stone hot-water bottle. He hadn't listened to the crystal set that night. There were too many thoughts buzzing around in his head. Bill couldn't believe that Sciver had finally been caught.

"If anything will give the boys a morale boost, it's that." Bill had clapped him on the back. "You deserve a medal, Tim. That's a real contribution to the war effort."

Tim snuggled into the pillow. The small, black,

transformer light hummed.

He awoke to voices in the upstairs hall. It must be really late, he thought. He remembered getting back into bed and lying awake for ages.

"I miss Will so much." Mum's voice was low, almost a whisper, but Tim could hear the break as she said Dad's name. "I almost thought it was him at the back door, I wanted to believe it so badly."

"I know, dear," said Grandma. "The Athelstan strain comes through so strongly in the boys. Look at Tim — just like Will at that age. And when I saw Bill, I almost thought the same myself." Grandma paused. "We mustn't stop praying."

Tim heard a long, low sigh and then his mother's voice. "I do, Mum, every night."

Chapter 25

Uncle Tom Cobley and All

Bill was gone. His visit the previous week, on Stir Up Sunday, had been his last. Two days later he returned to Canada to train new pilots and aircrew. Sparks had gone with him, as part of a training team.

Tim couldn't believe it. One minute Bill was here, the next he was gone. Why? Why did all the good things have to end? He'd thought Bill would be there for Christmas.

He sat on his bed, idly tuning the crystal set. He wasn't having much luck. All he could get were whistles and pops and crackling noises. He moved the cat's whisker. A voice came through faintly. It faded, and the earphones were filled instead with the loud screech of static. Tim took them off and put them on the eiderdown. He could still hear the abrasive, jarring electrical noise, but now he could also hear the drone of aircraft overhead. He got out of bed and went to the window, pushing his head beneath the curtains and blackout.

It was quite bright outside but difficult to see properly through the screen of lace curtaining stuck on the glass. There were traces of frost round the edges, too. He unlatched the side window and peered out. There were no tails of flame, no dragons in the sky. There hadn't been an alert in Medbury for ages. Since the Allies had captured the launch-sites in France, Hitler had been sending flying-bombs over from launch-pads in Holland, so they didn't fly over Medbury anymore.

The sky was clear, a mass of bright stars, each one blotted out and then reappearing as a stream of bombers thundered southward through the December night. Tim didn't watch for long. His feet were getting cold on the bare wood floor. The bombers were probably heading out to hit the V2 rocket launching sites. In the paper yesterday it said that Bomber Command had flown thirty missions last month against V2 targets. They had to get them! Seven hundred people had been killed the previous month and fifteen hundred injured from rocket attacks. Tim shut the window. It was cold, and he seemed to have lost interest in the planes since Bill had gone.

He waited until his eyes grew accustomed to the dim light in his room. Hanging from the ceiling was the flare parachute Bill had brought him.

Pinned to it, a dark spot against the white silk, was the penny Spitfire. On the eiderdown, the earphones crackled and whistled. Tim picked them up and sat on the edge of the bed. He wanted to hear the news. Was Hitler really dead? In yesterday's paper it said that not even the SS generals or the Nazi leaders knew what had happened to him. Tim moved the metal bead slowly along the coil. Nothing. He took off the headset and put it on his pillow. What was wrong? It was a beautiful clear night. The radio signals should be really strong.

He shivered and climbed into bed. Having the window open had made the room cold. He pulled up the covers. The stone hot-water bottle was still hot, but he wouldn't burn his feet if he took the cover off. He pulled the bottle up and undid the woollen cover Grandma Rose had made from one of Grandpa George's old socks. There was the shiny, brown, stoneware bottle. He thought of ginger beer. Maybe Grandpa Cecil could make a little for Christmas. The King had stood down the Home Guard yesterday, so Mum was going to ask Grandma Maude and Grandpa Cecil to come up from Eastbourne to spend Christmas at Bramley Cottage.

Tim smiled to himself. It would be nice to see Grandpa again. Sarah had thought that the photograph of the man in the paper, marching through Piccadilly, was Grandpa Cecil. He had the same kind of nose and the same bushy moustache. Even though it wasn't Grandpa, Sarah wanted to keep the picture.

There had been another photo, too. The King had presented a Canadian major with the V.C. for gallantry. To win the Victoria Cross was really something, but what had made Tim take notice was that the major had won it for bravery in Italy, in a battle over seven months ago. It reminded him of Dad. Dad had been fighting in Italy, he'd been mentioned in dispatches for bravery — that was ten months ago, and they still hadn't heard anything.

Tim sighed and turned on his back. He lay still. A voice came from the earphones on the pillow by his head. He reached up out of the warmth and put them on. There was a fierce crackle and then the voice returned, very clearly. It wasn't the news. It wasn't the BBC Home Service, it was a foreign voice. Tim struggled to sit up. It was a nuisance to have to tune the set now that he had a clear signal, but he couldn't understand a word the man was saying. The earphones went dead, and then, as he reached forward, the crackling started again. He reached up to take off the headset. There was a sharp click in the earphones and the voice came through clearly once more. The wire connection must be loose. Tim sat quite still and gently moved his hand until he could touch the wire where the headset was attached.

As he moved it there was a loud crackle. He took his hand away.

"And now for our English listeners, a song you all know well."

The voice had a heavy accent. It was the same man he'd heard before, here, and at Corvuston. The man began to sing:

"Tom Pearce, Tom Pearce, lend me your grey mare.
All along, down along, out along lea.
For I want to go to Widdecombe Fair,
With Will Athelstan, Tom Morse, David Hall, Edward Jones, Michael
Williams, Sam Dunn, old Uncle Tom Cobley and all, old Uncle —"

Tim ripped the headset off. His heart was racing as he jumped out of bed. Will Athelstan! That was Dad, Will Athelstan! "Mum!" he shouted. "Mum!" He ran into the hall.

"What on earth is all that noise?" Mum stood at the kitchen door, framed in the light. "What are you doing out of bed, Tim?"

"Mum. I heard Dad's name on the wireless!"

There was silence. Sarah's door opened wide. Tim felt that her eyes and Mum's eyes held him where he stood. Mum was silent. Then she spoke:

"What are you talking about, Tim?" Her voice was almost a whisper.

"On the wireless, Mum."

"You mean on that wretched crystal set? It's

long past eight o'clock. I knew I should have been more strict about that. Bring it down here, at once."

Tim hesitated. Then he continued. "You remember when I told you, when you were in the nursing home having baby Jane, at Corvuston, about Widdecombe Fair and Uncle Tom Cobley?"

Mum stared at him, her face drawn, her mouth a thin, pale line. "Please, Tim," she said quietly. "Please."

"But it's true, Mum. I did hear Dad's name." He nodded. "And, Mum, what was the name of Dad's sergeant?"

"Why? Why do you want to know that?"

"Because I think I heard his name, too."

Mum was staring at him, leaning against the doorpost. She sighed. "It was Sergeant Morse, Tim, now —"

"Tom Morse, Mum?"

Mum looked up sharply. "How did you know that? How did you know his name was Tom?"

"Because, Mum ... I told you. I heard his name too. I knew it. I knew it!" Tim ran into his bedroom, but the voice was no longer coming out of the headset, only piano music. He returned dejectedly into the hall.

Sarah was staring, first at him, and then at Mum, who was now coming up the stairs. Mum looked at him through the bannister rails.

"I did hear it, Mum." Tim felt like shouting. "Honestly, Mum. The man did sing Dad's name, only he said Vill Athelstan, not Will. Then he said Tom Morse and then some other names. I'm not lying, Mum."

Mum looked at him. "I believe you, Tim." There were tears running down her cheeks. "I do believe you. When you said Tom Morse, I knew."

Tim looked down at his feet. He wished Mum could have heard. "No one's singing anymore," he said, quietly. "It's just piano music." He looked up.

Mum was nodding, slowly. "I don't know what it means, Tim, but ..." She wiped her cheeks with a hanky. "Well, I've had a feeling, lately."

Six days later, the telegram arrived. It was date-stamped: 11DEC 44/LONDON W.C.

By Hand Delivery
Mrs. W. G. Athelstan
Bramley Cottage
Medbury, Nr. Tunbridge Wells

I am pleased to inform you that coded messages received from underground sources list Capt. W. G. Athelstan, Corps of Royal Engineers, as safe and in hiding. Radio communication from the same source confirms verbal messages. Further information cannot be given at this time, but particulars will be forwarded as soon as possible
Under Secretary of State for War.

Tim watched his mother's face as she read out the news. She was blinking back tears and her voice shook, but her eyes shone with a light he hadn't seen for a long time. Dad might not be home in time for Christmas, but the news was the best present anyone could have.

"Tom Pearce, Tom Pearce, lend me your grey mare." Tim found himself humming the tune to himself. It wasn't a Christmas carol, but he was sure he'd remember it every Christmas from now on. *"Will Athelstan, Enid Athelstan, Tim Athelstan, Sarah Athelstan, Jane Athelstan, old Uncle Tom Cobley and all, old Uncle Tom Cobley and all."*